GET
RICH
QUICK

B stands for Brainwaves, because in this club you do two things: one, you have a brainwave; two, you carry it out. Most of the brainwaves are to do with earning money but sometimes they're about important missions we have to do – special investigations and things like that. The other reason for calling it the B Club is because of all the code words we invent beginning with B, like blimp and blatant.

Anyway, I joined Shane and Jammy in the shed and told them my brilliant idea about the invention to get rich quick.

Please see page 196 for a glossary to look up the B Club's B words!

Ann Bryant

Hippo

Scholastic Children's Books,
Scholastic Publications Ltd,
7–9 Pratt Street, London NW1 0AE, UK

Scholastic Inc.,
555 Broadway, New York, NY 10012-3999, USA

Scholastic Canada Ltd,
123 Newkirk Road, Richmond Hill,
Ontario, Canada L4C 3G5

Ashton Scholastic Pty Ltd,
PO Box 579, Gosford, New South Wales,
Australia

Ashton Scholastic Ltd,
Private Bag 94407, Greenmount, Auckland,
New Zealand

First published in the UK by Scholastic Publications Ltd, 1995

Copyright © Ann Bryant, 1995

ISBN 0 590 55933 8

Typeset by DP Photosetting, Aylesbury, Bucks

Printed by Cox & Wyman Ltd, Reading, Berks

10 9 8 7 6 5 4 3 2 1

Contents

For Jody and Carly

1

The B Club

It was a typical Saturday morning. Mum was busy carting armloads of scrumpled sheets, towels and clothes from bedroom to bedroom and then heaving them all downstairs for the wash.

"Right. That's that done," she said in a busy, bright voice. Then she called out to me, "Tim, I'm just popping down to Pat's, love, for a quick coffee – about an hour, okay?"

Well, she'd only been gone about five minutes when I decided to go down to Jammy's. I'd just thought of this great new word for our B Club – *blimp*. It means forget whatever it is you're doing, because it's useless. It just came into my head when I was doing my maths homework. Question Four was impossible so I decided to blimp the whole thing and go to Jammy's. I thought I ought to tell Mum where I was going so I went round to Pat's.

It only takes a couple of minutes to get to Pat's. Her back door was slightly ajar and I could hear them talking.

"Well, you're surely not *that* short, Marg, are you?" Pat was saying to Mum.

"We are, I'm afraid; it's horrendous," Mum said.

"Pity you can't invent something and get rich quick," suggested Pat, and Mum laughed.

"I was thinking about Marks and Spencer's actually. Well, it's either that or rob a bank," Mum answered.

Rob a bank! Mum, robbing a bank! Or

lifting stuff from Marks and Spencer's! I decided not to tell anyone what I'd heard except the bit about inventing something and getting rich quick. That sounded like a good idea.

"Any news on the bookshop?" Pat was saying to Mum. Her voice seemed to be getting louder. Course it was; she was coming towards the back door, wasn't she? I quickly bent my knees, just enough to stop my head showing through the glass bit at the top. I didn't want them to know I'd been listening.

"Hello, Tim. What are you doing here?" said Pat, reaching past my bent legs for a pint of milk.

Well honestly, I must have looked absolutely blatant. (Blatant was Jammy's invention, by the way. It means really stupid and embarrassing. Jammy's usually pretty blatant himself, so thinking that up was a step in the right direction for him.)

"I was just in the middle of bending down

when my knees went all stiff," I said to Pat, and she made a funny noise as though her knees were hurting too. "Oh, Tim, are they all right now?"

"Yes, they're fine now. The click's gone out of them."

I stood up straight and she called over her shoulder, "Marg, Tim's here." Then to me, "Come in; I was just about to make the coffee."

"'S all right, I was just going to say something to Mum. Going up to Jammy's, Mum. Okay?"

"Okay. Lunch at one."

"Yeah. Bye!"

I sprinted down to Jammy's. His real name is Nicholas. We call him Jammy because he gets all the jammy jobs to do at school, like missing bits of lessons by taking messages to other teachers. There's a great way to stop him getting cocky about it. Just write KNICKERLESS on his maths homework book, but don't forget to write in capitals. (It's harder to detect handwriting patterns if you write in capitals.)

Jammy lives in a cul-de-sac, which means bum of bag in French. So we call Jammy's cul-de-sac Bumbag Road. I found him and Shane in the shed in Jammy's garden. Shane's in the B Club too.

There are just the three of us although loads of other people would like to join, but we haven't found any of them suitable. B stands for Brainwaves, because in this club you do two things: one, you have a brainwave; two, you carry it out. Most of the brainwaves are to do with earning money but sometimes they're about important missions we have to do – special investigations and things like that. It's very difficult to get new members to realize the importance of top-secret work, that's why the club has limited its membership to me, Jammy and Shane. We understand these things, you see. Well, Shane and I do, and Jammy *tries* to understand. The other reason for calling it the B Club is because of all the code words we invent beginning with B, like blimp and blatant.

Anyway, I joined Shane and Jammy in the shed and told them my brilliant idea about the invention to get rich quick.

"Burnt out!" said Jammy. (That means really impressive, Shane thought of that one.)

"Right, what shall we invent?" asked Shane, tapping his finger on his chin like a businessman working on an executive decision. Shane's always fancied himself in big business.

"It's got to be something that's never been invented before," said Jammy, whose brain-waves are usually painfully slow.

"Course it's got to be something that's never been invented before, otherwise it wouldn't be an invention," said Shane in an insulting gormless voice. Then he carried on in his proper voice, "Anyway, I vote something for housework because all women will want one then."

"Right," I said. "A household item. All shut your eyes and think hard what your mum hasn't got that she could really do with."

So we all shut our eyes and sniggered. Then we opened them again and said lots of stupid things like Kylie Minogue's legs.

"Right, now serious things," I said, and we stayed silent for ages.

"Oh, let's forget it," said Shane after a bit.

"No, hang on a sec, what about a laundry carrier? Like a ball that you shove your towels and sheets and things into, then roll it downstairs to the washing machine."

For about twenty seconds Shane and Jammy stared straight ahead thinking about my plan, then Jammy spoke.

"Burnt out!"

"So how do we make it?" asked Shane.

"First we've got to design it," I explained. "So all go home, write down how big it should be, what it should be made of and all that stuff, then meet here at four o'clock."

"Then we take it to the patent place, they look in their book to check no one else thought of it first, then they pay us loads of money," added Shane, who thinks he knows everything.

When I got home I found Mum in the kitchen, bending down to look under the eye-level grill.

"Just in time, just done the side twos," she said, briskly whipping the toasts out from under the grill. "Lots of beans? Few beans?" she said, spoon hovering. "How hungry are you?"

"Quite."

"Quite a few beans then," and she tipped the whole lot on to the two toasts.

"Actually," I said, wondering how she'd get round this one, "lots of beans."

She didn't say anything, just scraped a few dried-up beans from the side of the pan on to the steaming heap. I grinned at her but she didn't get it.

"Mum?"

"Mmmm."

"I've invented a ball thing to get your washing downstairs in."

"What a coincidence!"

"What?"

"Nothing, love. Carry on about the ball."

"Well, what should I make it out of?"

"Plastic, I should think. It would need to be very light."

"Yeah. How big do you think?"

"Let's see, how do you measure a sphere? You'd need to know the diameter ... um ... one metre? Slightly more?"

"Great! Thanks, Mum."

While I was scoffing my beans I was thinking where I'd get all the plastic from and how I'd make it into an exact sphere.

"You'd need to be able to open it, Tim."

"Yes, you would," I said, feeling quite

pleased that she was so interested in my invention.

"I think a flap would be the best idea, perhaps with a zip."

I ate my beans as fast as I could, then went upstairs and sat at my desk drawing diagrams of the laundry ball.

Mum called upstairs, "Tim, I'm just going down to Marks and Spencer's. I'll be back before tea, okay?"

"Okay," I said, trying to sound normal when I was actually dead shocked. Mum really *was* going to rob Marks and Spencer's. I'd better stop her, and fast!

Marks and Spencer's in our town is pretty big – six doors to choose from. I went in through the fourth one. I wandered through Children's Knitwear, looking casually at the odd jumper and the occasional pair of socks, trying to look normal. Then I came to Ladies'

Underwear – Lingerie, it said. I went quickly through that bit and just stared straight ahead.

Guess who was standing by one of the food checkouts? Mum. There was a man right next to her. I began to feel a bit funny. I never really thought Mum would try anything but it was looking horribly as though I was wrong. I got as close as I could behind some ladies' jackets and saw the man put his hand on Mum's arm.

"If you'd like to come along with me, Mrs Scragg," he was saying, "the store manager's office is at the back here."

And he started to lead Mum away.

It must take guts to try shoplifting. Poor old Mum, great on guts but blatant on skill. So here she was getting carted away to the manager's office by a store detective. My brain didn't have time for a proper plan. I just whizzed right up to that detective, shook his arm and said, "Look over there – someone's nicking something!" That gave Mum a chance to run, but she just stood there looking red and funny.

"What ... are ... you ... doing ... here, Tim?" she asked, with her lips tight like a ventriloquist. I didn't answer because the store detective had legged it right across the store to the six doors, and was talking to a lad called Pushty from our school.

Oh, God! I couldn't have picked a worse person. Pushty was older than me and big for his age with greasy black hair, black eyes and a slimy sort of face. Hardly anybody liked him and most people were scared of him, including me. Mum and I watched in silence. Pushty had his hands on his hips and his legs apart. He was staring back at me. The store detective was lurching back to me and Mum.

"False alarm, actually," he said to me, pleasantly enough. "Well spotted though. The jumper is his own; he got it from our Bradford Branch. When you get close you can see it's quite an old one. Nothing like that in *our* stocks, I hope!"

He laughed jovially and Mum laughed in unusual gulps.

"Now, if you'll excuse me . . ." He turned to Mum. "Sorry about the slight delay. Let's go and see about the job, shall we?"

I tried a smile at Mum but I didn't get one back so I looked at my watch. Ten to four. Pushty was nowhere in sight so I thought it was probably safe to leave.

I said "Bradford Branch" to myself all the way to Jammy's, thinking I'd use that from now on as the B Club's way of saying a really good ending.

"Where's yours, Tim?" asked Jammy, as I sat down in his shed.

"My what?"

"Invention," said Shane in a gormless voice.

"At home, actually," I said, "but I've invented a new word – Bradford Branch. It means a lucky ending. You know, getting out of a tight squeeze with a good result."

Shane said things like "Wonderful" and "Oh, yes, really useful" until my ears felt hot. I'd completely forgotten about the invention.

"Anyway, let's look at yours then," I said, trying for a sneery-sounding tone.

"Oh, we're not bothering. It was a stupid idea," said Shane.

"It's impossible to make a ball," Jammy explained slowly. "It's got no sides. You can't hammer it or stick it or anything, so it's impossible."

"Well, *I've* done it," I said, without really thinking that one through.

"Let's see then."

"I told you, it's not properly finished. It takes time, you know. Anyway, I'm going back to work on it. See you tomorrow!"

I knew Mum hadn't got the job as soon as I walked through the back door. She was sitting with her shoulders hunched and she didn't look round when I went in.

"Hi, Mum. Sorry about the mistake. You see, I thought you were ... well, did you get it? The job?"

She sighed and sort of smiled.

"I didn't take it. The hours were too long. Anyway, I would have had to do Saturdays." She looked at me with her chin resting on her hand, her elbow propped on the table.

"Tim, tell me, did you really think that boy was pinching a sweater?"

"No, I thought ... that bloke was arresting you for shoplifting."

"You *what?*" Mum suddenly cracked up laughing. "Wait till I tell Pat," she spluttered.

"But I heard you and Pat talking about it — *and* the bank robbery ..."

"You are priceless!" she said, slapping her hands down on the table. "Absolutely priceless! We were joking." Then she suddenly sounded all bright and busy again. "Guess what I've done?"

I sat down and she told me how she'd written down all about my sheet ball and sent it off to a competition in *Every Woman's Dream* magazine "for an invention to help with a common household task."

"Look," she said, skimming the magazine across the table to me, "a hundred pounds prize money!" We looked at each other.

"Wow! Could be all right, Mum!"

2

Budding Blues Artist

It was school the next day but I didn't really mind because there were only two days before the end of term, and anyway I was feeling quite buzzy (excited and busy at the same time).

"Get rich quick!" I kept saying it over and over again, in different voices. Sometimes I used different accents like Scottish and Australian.

On Monday morning I left my hymn book in the school assembly hall and had to go back for it. The hall was huge and silent. It seemed to be waiting for me. The stage seemed to be waiting for me too. All the teachers were safely in their classrooms so I climbed the few steps and stood right at the front, centre stage.

"Good morning, everybody." I paused for the answer then continued in a deeper voice, "This morning we will sing hymn number sixty-one."

I nodded at Miss Ridge at the piano and she began to play. Funny though, what she was playing wasn't hymn sixty-one at all, it was the blues. It was absolutely bandy (Jammy's word for burnt-out music)! I just had to start singing so I grabbed the mike and gave my best performance with a good strong American accent:

"You know it makes me SICK – SICK – SICK
The way I see you GET – RICH – QUICK!
I said SICK – SICK – SICK – YEAH!
I said GET – RICH – QUICK – YEAH!

You know it makes me SPEW – SPEW –
  SPEW
The way I'm not as RICH – AS – YOU!
I said SPEW – SPEW – SPEW – YEAH!
I said RICH – AS – YOU – YEAH!

You know it makes me PUKE – PUKE –
  PUKE
I'll never be a PRINCE – OR – DUKE!
I said PUKE – PUKE – PUKE – YEAH!
I said PRINCE – OR – DUKE – YEAH!

You know it makes me —"

"Tim!"

"BORGONZOLA!"

"Tim, what *are* you doing up there? I
thought you were ill for a moment."

"Nothing, miss."

It gave me quite a shock to see old Rigid
Bottom looking up at me. (Borgonzola is what
you say when you're in shock, you see.) I was

19

still imagining her belting out the blues on the piano. She was sort of half smiling.

"Well, I wouldn't describe it as nothing — flinging yourself around that stage like a thing possessed!"

Then she broke into one of those stupid secretive smiles that women put on for little kids, but I forgave her because she obviously liked my song.

"Very good, Tim, apart from the words. And don't worry," she went on in a voice that exactly matched the smile, "I won't tell anyone you're a budding blues artist."

"I came in for my hymn book, miss. It's not up here, so I'll look down there," I mumbled.

"You do that," she said, and vanished.

It's funny how things stick in your head. "Budding blues artist" — I couldn't get that unstuck all day or the next.

"Mum," I asked the next evening, "have you got any blues cassettes?"

"Blues? No, sorry ... oh, Tim, by the way, I thought I'd take on a lodger – you know, for the money really. How would you feel about that?"

"Fine."

I went upstairs and mimed hard to "Checkin' it Out" by Ricky Stone. It didn't look right with my school uniform on so I changed into my jeans and an unbuttoned shirt. My chest looked very pale, and I thought I might improve the chest and the general atmosphere with a little less light. I turned the light off and couldn't see a thing. A spotlight was what I really needed. My bedside lamp on the edge of the wardrobe looked demon, and I did a whole Ricky Stone concert followed by a load of autograph signing till bedtime. I lay in bed listening to the clapping and couldn't wait to tell Shane and Jammy my plan.

*   *   *

"A group?" said Jammy, sprinkling hamster food all over the hamster on the first day of our Easter holidays. "Don't be daft, we don't know any music."

"We haven't got any guitars or drums or anything," said Shane.

"A singing group," I told them patiently, and waited for it to sink in.

"Blimpworthy," pronounced Shane. "Sorry, Tim, but that is totally blimpworthy, I'm afraid."

I looked at Jammy. Jammy looked at Shane. Shane carried on.

"You can't just sing. You need music, you need a band," he said.

"I'll sing on my own then," I said, slamming the shed door. "Look out for the name – Bill Brent," I called through the door. "That's going to be my stage name so look out for it."

I heard Shane snigger.

"In lights," I added as I walked off.

> *Dear Jim,*
> *Please could you fix it for me to sing on a stage at my very own concert with my name up in lights somewhere everyone can see it . . .*

I read through what I had written and nearly screwed the letter up. It suddenly seemed a pretty kiddish thing to do, writing to *Jim'll Fix It*. Jimmy Saville probably wouldn't choose my letter anyway. Lots of people wanted to sing on the stage. I thought I ought to make sure my letter stood out from all the others. I started again.

> *Dear Jim,*
> *Please please could you fix it for me to sing a solo. My music teacher said she thought I was possessed of a really good voice . . .*

After all, Miss Ridge had said something about being possessed, hadn't she? But that still wouldn't be enough to get singled out. I'd somehow have to prove I was a really bandy singer. Perhaps I could write out some lyrics in the letter.

> *Dear Jim,*
> *My music teacher heard me sing.*
> *She said I was possessed.*
> *She said my voice was heaven sent*
> *And I was heaven blessed.*
> *She said I ought to write to you*
> *And hope you'd do the rest.*
> *So please please PLEASE fix it for me to sing*
> *my songs in my own concert.*
> *from*
> *Bill Brent*

Uh-oh! There was something else I'd forgotten. I didn't want to wait for months while Jimmy Saville worked his way through loads of other people's fix-its, so I added a quick note to clinch it.

> *P.S. Better hurry, my voice feels like*
> *it's going to break any minute.*

A feeling of excitement crept to the front of my brain and popped out of my head the next morning. My singing career was about to be launched. I would need to look good. Getting dressed and eating my breakfast I imagined my audience: talent-spotters, autograph-hunters, Mum, Shane, Jammy – and *no way* Pushty.

"I think I need some more clothes, Mum," I commented, trying to sound casual with a big piece of toast in my mouth.

"Don't speak with your mouth full, Tim. How often have I got to tell you?"

I tried again without any toast and it didn't sound very casual at all.

"You had new jeans, a shirt, sweater and trainers at the beginning of the holidays. You know I'm short at the moment. You'll just have to make do with what you've got – unless of course you get yourself a little job. Why not pop up to Levins and see if they want someone to deliver newspapers?"

"They don't need anyone. Dentures works for them."

"Dentures? What an unfortunate name."

"That's because he's got unfortunate teeth. Jammy reckons he carries the papers in his teeth so he's got both hands free for his bike. You should see them, Mum – they stick out so much, his top lip nearly blocks his nostrils off!"

"Don't make fun of people, Tim. What about washing people's cars? I'm sure you'd get the odd pound if you asked politely and not too often. Green Lane would be a good place to start."

"Okay. I'll give it a go."

Mum patted my shoulder and smiled with her head on one side. "Things won't always be this tight, Tim. I'm taking over from Teresa Mulgrew at the bookshop when she goes into hospital next week, *and –*" Mum did a big smile and put her hands on both my shoulders – "the new lodger's coming this morning for a chat."

"Oh, great news!" I said sarcastically. "Someone's coming to live in our house and share *our* bathroom and *our* food, are they?" I was cross that she'd arranged it without asking me first.

"Well, it's not definite yet," said Mum, who must have thought I'd be as thrilled as she obviously was at the thought of a complete stranger in the house. "I'm seeing him today, to see how we get on ..."

"Him! It's a bloke, is it? Thanks for letting me know."

"Oh, come on, that's not fair. I've mentioned it several times but you've never seemed interested. Look, why don't you make sure you're here at twelve o'clock? Then you can meet him. He sounded very nice in his letter. He's going to teach French at Maverleys."

"A teacher! I don't want a teacher in the

house. I see enough of them at school without coming home to one every day."

"Well, it's not like having one from the same school as yours. You never know, he may be able to help you with your French homework."

"I'll go and see about washing cars, I think."

"See you at twelve then – oh, and be polite, won't you?"

I wasn't sure if she meant to the car owners or the French teacher, but I didn't particularly feel like being polite to anyone.

There was a postbox on the way to Green Lane. I posted my *Jim'll Fix It* letter in slow motion, saying "Good luck will come to Timothy Scragg" as I dropped it in.

A voice behind me made me jump.

"Hello, Timothy. Been writing letters, have we?"

It was Pushty. He sounded as though he meant business.

"Just one letter actually," I stammered.

"Well, that was a pretty nasty trick you played on me in Marks and Spencer's," he said in a slow, threatening voice.

"I didn't realize it was you, honestly, Pushty."

"So who's the letter to?" he went on horribly.

"Umm, Jimmy Saville," I admitted, a little shamefacedly.

"Jimmy Saville, eh? And what's it about, Timothy Scragg?"

I didn't dare tell a lie. There's something about Pushty that makes you think twice before telling a lie.

"It's about me singing a song," I said.

"How sweet," said Pushty with a horrid false smile. "Little Tim wants to be a singer."

He laughed as he strolled away.

My heartbeat gradually slowed down.

3

The Lodger

By the time I'd got to Green Lane I'd forgotten all about Pushty. The people who lived in Green Lane had amazing cars. Mum reckoned you could buy a whole house for the money some of those cars cost. Let's hope they'd be in their garages looking mucky and awful, their owners just dying for someone like me to come along and clean them so they could leave them on show in their drives.

I began to feel excited thinking of all the money I was about to make. I could feel another great blues song coming on ...

I'm going to shine your car, yeah!
Wash away that grime,
Going to do it twice a week
For two pounds every time.
Going to make a fortune,
Going to make my name.
Timothy Scragg grabs that rag,
Rubs that jag and rises to fame!

Bandy! I tried to sing it again but I couldn't remember it. It looked like I was probably going to be a singer/songwriter, the way I made things up just like that. I'd have to get some new batteries for my tape recorder and take it with me everywhere I went so I could record all my compositions.

Meanwhile there were fifteen cars waiting for me. I thought it might be worth singing the song as I washed each car, then if a talent spotter happened to be listening I could kill two birds with one stone – get paid for the car wash and rise to fame faster.

I kicked a stone with my left foot and it rolled for ages. A car was drawing up on the pavement right alongside it and I watched as the pebble trickled a little further than the car. That gave me an idea. I waited until I heard another car coming then kicked another pebble, hard. I said to myself, if the pebble is still rolling when the car's gone past it means I'll get fifteen cars to clean.

I held my breath and willed the car to go faster, but unfortunately the pebble stopped first.

"Right," I said, "this time if the pebble beats the car it means I'll get *ten* cars to clean. I found a good big stone, waited till I heard a car coming, then kicked as hard as I could. The pebble hit a lamppost and stopped straight away. Another loser. Okay, this is for *five* cars to clean. I cheated a bit by kicking the stone quite a few seconds after I heard a car approaching.

Unfortunately, I looked up and my foot

missed the stone altogether and I kicked mid-air, which made me feel really blatant because two girls in the car turned round and grinned out of the back window as if to say, "What a blanko!" (That's what the B Club call anyone who does something totally blatant.)

I was pretty fed up by then I can tell you, so I kicked the last stone really hard, thinking, "Right, this is for *no* cars to clean." The stone rolled and rolled and rolled, long after the car had gone by.

'S only rubbish anyway, I thought, as I rang the first bell. There was a smart Mercedes in the drive.

"I wonder if I could possibly wash your Mercedes for you?" I politely asked the tall lady who answered the door. She stank of perfume so much I had to hold my breath.

"Does it look as though it needs a wash?" she asked crisply.

"Well, not really . . . I just —"

"No, thank you." And she shut the door in my face.

The next house had four milk bottles on the doorstep and I knew before I'd even pressed the bell that there would be no answer. The house after that had quite a dirty-looking cream-coloured Volvo estate in the drive. It also had a fierce-looking pair of Alsatians in the drive. When they noticed me they leapt up at the gate, teeth bared, throats gurgling. I kept hoping they'd bark. That at least would attract the owner's attention, but they just went on quietly snarling, so I moved on to the next house ... and the next ... and the next ...

No luck with any of them. No one in. I suppose Wednesday morning isn't the best time in the world to find cars to clean, I thought angrily. But then another thought occurred to me – rather a bangler. (That means a sudden good thought just popping into your head, like when you wake up and start getting your school uniform on and suddenly remember it's the weekend. That's the bangler coming into your head.)

I was pretty puffed when I got to Jammy's shed and then dead disappointed to find no one there.

"In here, Tim," called Jammy.

"Behind the roses," added Shane helpfully.

They'd made a camp there. It wasn't bad.

"You look like you've won the pools," said Shane, as I squatted in the camp.

"Better than that," I told him. "I'm *psychic*!"

"What's that?" asked Jammy. "Is it catching?"

"It's when you know things that other people don't know."

"What, like being really clever?" asked Jammy.

"No, more than that. It's brainwaves seeing into the future and knowing things you've never been told."

I explained to them how the pebbles showed I wasn't going to get a single car to clean, and how that turned out to be exactly right.

"That doesn't prove anything," said Shane grumpily when I'd finished. Shane can't bear to think he's not the best at anything. "Bet it wouldn't work if you tried it now."

"Lu-unch, Nicholas!" called Jammy's mum.

I looked at my watch. It said quarter past twelve.

"Got to go. Sorry. S'posed to be meeting our new lodger."

"Oh, yeah," said Shane sarcastically. "Very convenient."

"No, honestly. Mum said be back at twelve."

"What's he like then, your new lodger?"

"How should I know? I've never met him."

"Yeah, but if you were psychic you'd know, wouldn't you?"

We all three looked at each other.

"I'll tell Mum to hang on for five minutes," said Jammy. "Come on, let's do the pebble-kicking test to see what he looks like."

So we all trooped out on to the street and waited for a car to come by. After about three minutes when no cars had gone by, Shane pointed out that Jammy's cul-de-sac wasn't the best place in the world to wait for cars to go by.

"Okay, just kick pebbles and see how far they go," said Jammy, which was quite a sensible suggestion for Jammy. He was probably panicking about being late for lunch. He always thinks better under pressure, does Jammy.

"If the pebble goes past that white gate it means he's fat. If it doesn't go that far it means he's thin," I said.

I closed my eyes and kicked. When I opened them again the pebble was just trickling up to the gatepost, and someone was standing at the end of Bumbag Road watching us. Shane hadn't noticed.

"Not fat, not thin, just medium," he pronounced.

I nudged Shane and jerked my head towards the person at the end of the road.

"What's the matter? Are your brainwaves jumping about?" asked Jammy, looking quite concerned.

"Look!" I hissed, jerking my head with a bit more vigour.

Jammy screwed up his eyes and looked. "That's Lisa Farrant," he announced casually. "She's nice," he added.

Shane eyed the distant figure and raised one corner of his lip, which made his nose wrinkle, as though Jammy had just dropped into the conversation that Pushty was nice.

"Never mind *her*," Shane said disdainfully. "This is much more important. Right, now do tall or short. Past the gatepost means tall, not up to it, short."

I shut my eyes and kicked again. When I opened them I saw the pebble trickle just past the gatepost.

"A bit on the tall side," stated Shane. "Now dark or fair," he carried on. "Past the gatepost means dark —"

"Not up to the gatepost, fair," Jammy finished off, looking proud of himself because he'd just caught on.

This time when I opened my eyes the pebble was still rolling quite hard. It went past the gatepost and nearly as far as the next one! Jammy and Shane gazed after it long after it had stopped rolling.

"Perhaps he's black," said Shane.

"Well, he's certainly dark," I said. "I'll see you later," I called, as Jammy ran into his house and Shane stood frowning at the pebble.

"Meet you at the camp at two o'clock," said Shane. "And he'd better be medium fat, quite tall and pretty dark, or you're dead."

I ran all the way home, noticing on the way that Lisa Farrant had done a disappearing act. I was half hoping I'd be too late to meet the lodger, but I knew I wasn't as soon as I came round the bend into our road. There was a blue Fiesta parked right outside our house. I pushed open the gate and belted round the side of the house and into the kitchen through the back door. Mum was drinking tea with the new lodger.

"Oh, this is my son Timothy," said Mum.

The man stood up and held out his hand. I just stared. I was totally borgonzola-ed. He was medium fat, quite tall, and with that dark foreign skin made even darker because he'd obviously been in the sun.

"Tim, this is Monsieur Caviézel, our new lodger."

I don't know how long I gawped at the Frenchman. It was like a dream, but when I woke I realized my fingers had been crunched by his strong handshake.

"No, no pliss, not Monsieur Caviézel. I am François Bernard," (he pronounced it *France wa Bear Nar*), "and to my friends just Bernard (*Bear-Nar*), and I am hoping we shall be friends, hein?"

He was smiling and nodding at me and Mum alternately during this speech, but I had a job following what he was saying partly because of his French accent (I made a note to sing my next made-up song with a French accent) and partly because I was so excited. I mean, there was no doubting my psychic powers now. The pebble had definitely got its facts right. Just like Shane said — medium fat, quite tall and pretty dark.

"Well, Bear Nar," Mum was saying, sounding like she was straight out of an episode of *Allo Allo*, "what about another cup of tea?" She pointed to the pot, and in a slow, loud, embarrassing voice, said, "Tea? More? For you?"

Bear Nar just laughed.

"Meessees Scragg," he said as he sat down again, "I would lurv more tea, if eet ees not trurble."

"Oh, call me Margery, please."

"Of course, Marrrrrgery," he said, rolling the r's around in his mouth for a while.

I'd had enough of Mum's pink face by then, and couldn't wait to tell Jammy and Shane about Bear Nar.

"Mum, I'm supposed to be cleaning a car up at Green Lane. I'd better go."

"But what about lunch, Tim? And *you'll* stay, will you, Bear Nar? Stay for lunch?" Mum started nodding and smiling as though she was giving Bear Nar a clue that the answer was yes.

"Delighted, but pliss nurting spessial for me."

"No trouble at all," said Mum, sounding really stupid.

I pulled the back door shut behind me.

4

Signor Psychic Scraggini

About five minutes later Jammy's back door was opened by his mum.

"Well, that was quick," she said, when she saw who it was. "Nicholas'll be at least another twenty minutes, Tim. He's helping me with Dora at the moment."

Dora was Jammy's little sister. I think she was nearly two. She must have heard her name because she appeared at the door with no clothes on except a bib. There was lots of banana and carrot and dribble and milk on the bib. It looked really disgusting. Then Jammy appeared with a spoon and went red when he saw me. He tried to hide the spoon behind his back.

"Won't be a minute, Tim," he said.

What happened next was almost as amazing as me being psychic. Lisa Farrant suddenly popped up behind Jammy.

"Hello, Tim," she said with a smile. Jammy's face was so red he could have been understudying for a giant tomato if you'd cut his body off.

My eyes must have said, "What's *she* doing here?" because Jammy said, "Lisa's just helping Mum with Dora."

Good. That was okay. At least she was just helping Jammy's mum. But then Lisa spoke and ruined my day.

"It's great fun, Tim," she said. "Jammy and I have been taking it in turns to put a spoonful of food into Dora's mouth. We laid bets on which one of us could feed her the most spoonfuls, because sometimes she just pushes the spoon away, doesn't she, Jammy?"

Jammy didn't answer because he wasn't there. He'd disappeared with his stupid tomato face.

Lisa shrugged and smiled at me but I didn't smile back, 'cause she made me sick.

I decided to go round to Shane's place. One of his older sisters opened the door and looked very disappointed when she saw me.

"Is Shane in, please?" I asked.

She didn't answer, just looked down at the step then walked back into her house with a very bored look on her face as though I was a big bluebottle that had accidentally bashed into the door, knocked itself out and was lying dead on the doorstep. I was just wondering whether the open door meant I could go inside, when Shane appeared.

"Hi!"

I followed him in.

"What's he look like then, your lodger?"

"Sit down, Tim," said Mrs Plant, who always looked amused for some reason when she saw me. The table was covered with plates and knives, butter, cheese, biscuits and bread, and loads of crumbs. Round the table sat Mr and Mrs Plant, Claire Plant (the one who'd answered the door), Sheena Plant (who looked about nineteen or something), and Douglas Plant (who looked a bit older than Claire, probably about seventeen).

Shane's family aren't like other families, partly because it's more like five grown-ups and one child. The five grown-ups do lots of joking and laughing and nobody ever seems to argue. I think Shane feels a bit left out because he doesn't get the jokes. So he pretends to be really cool and businesslike and that only makes them laugh even more.

I've decided I'll have lots of private jokes with my wife when I get married, only I'll make sure the children understand so they can join in.

I just wished Shane hadn't asked about Bear Nar in front of all his family. Something told me they were going to be pretty sarcastic about pebble-kicking having anything to do with our lodger's looks.

"Come on, Tim, what does he look like? Is he fat or thin?" asked Mr Plant, with a teeny wink at Mrs Plant which he must have thought I was too blind to see. The whole family was looking at me with the same amused faces.

"Medium," I mumbled and Shane's eyes widened.

"Tall or short?" asked Douglas Plant, leaning forward as though it was really interesting. I could tell he was just pretending.

"Quite tall," I answered as casually as possible. Shane stood up dramatically and asked me the last question in slow motion as though the future of the world depended on my answer.

"Dark or fair?"

I was looking forward to the Plants wiping the smiles off their faces when they heard this!

"Very very dark!"

Shane gasped. "Burnt out!" he breathed with a big grin on his face, then he put his arm round my shoulder.

"Tim is going into business. Signor Psychic Scraggini!" he announced. "And I am going to be his business manager."

He looked round at everyone then back at me. "Come on, Tim, let's get organized."

No one round that table said a single word, but I could see eyes shooting from side to side and lips tightening. I noticed Douglas puffing out his cheeks and a funny noise slipped out of his mouth. He looked as though he was in agony trying not to laugh.

"See you later, Mum," said Shane, who hadn't noticed anything odd.

His mother just nodded. Her eyes were watering.

When we got to Shane's front gate we

heard a great explosive noise coming from his kitchen. They were all laughing their heads off. I could just imagine them round the table, clutching their stomachs and rocking backwards and forwards, but still Shane didn't notice. Perhaps he was used to them laughing at him. I'd hate to be Shane. It must be awful to be the youngest in a big family — much better to be the only one. Jammy's quite lucky though. I suppose I wouldn't mind a little sister, but I'd never tell anyone that. It's private.

You should have seen Jammy's shed. It was like a proper studio. In fact I was seriously thinking of becoming a famous artist. We were painting the posters and they looked great. It took us all afternoon to do three and we'd still got three more to do.

I think Neptune and Jupiter must have crossed each other on a creative path running right through the middle of my birth sign, I was feeling so good. Great painter, talented songwriter, demon psychic.

There was only one thing spoiling my good mood and that was the thought of Jammy being with that girl. Jammy even had the cheek to ask if silly little Lisa Farrant could join our B Club.

"No!" I said. "Definitely not! For three reasons: 1) she's boring, 2) she's bossy and 3) she's blatant."

Jammy said, "Only asking," and did this shuffling thing with his feet that he does when he's trying to think of something good to say.

Anyway, apart from the odd bodger (bad thought) about Jammy and that girl, it was buzz buzz buzz in that shed.

Each poster said my name (SIGNOR PSYCHIC SCRAGGINI), where to find me (KENNEL WOODS), and how much it cost to have your fortune read (three pounds fifty). We were going to say 35p, but Shane said,

"Cut it, kids. *I'm* the business manager, and I say ten times as much as that."

We worked out that ten thirty-fives were three hundred and fifty. Jammy said he thought three hundred and fifty pounds was probably a bit too much to ask, so we settled on three pounds fifty.

I'm going to be so rich, even after I've given Shane his cut. Jammy's going to take money at the door so he'll probably take his own cut. Well, it's not exactly a door, more of a fir tree really. You see I'm going to be sitting in this camp we made in Kennel Woods. It's really brilliant. We used loads of sheets from Shane's house for the walls (his mum hasn't even noticed they're missing), and two table-cloths (which my mum never uses) for the carpets.

The next day we finished the posters and put them up on lampposts all over the place, then we rushed into Kennel Woods and I sat on the carpet with my legs crossed. I was wearing a big jacket with sequins on it from Shane's sister's wardrobe, and a glittery headband thing round my head from his other sister's top drawer. I also had a mask over my eyes from Jammy's dressing-up box. I looked really Spanish or Italian or whatever I was supposed to be. Pinned to the fir tree was a card which said HAVE YOUR FORTUNE READ HERE.

Shane reckoned I needed a sort of crystal ball. I wasn't going to use it or anything but it would give atmosphere and a psychic look to the camp. We couldn't find anything crystal and sphere-shaped until Jammy's guinea pig belted into the sitting room in this big plastic ball, so we took that, and it looked quite good on the carpet with rusty leaves spread out all round it in a diamond pattern. We decided to tell all the people who came to have their fortunes told that the diamond points repre-sented the forces of good, evil, rich and poor.

That was one of the ideas I had when I was feeling buzzy in Jammy's shed.

It was two o'clock in the afternoon on Good Friday when we got settled in the camp. We called it the Psychic Camp at first (you pronounce psychic like this – sigh kick) so after a bit we just said Kick Camp for short.

I had a whole bucketful of pebbles ready to roll on the carpet. What I planned to do was to tell the person to ask a question, then I'd announce the rules for the pebble, roll the pebble, see how far it went and tell the person the answer.

For example if one of the Green Lane people came in and wanted to know how rich they'd be in five years' time, I'd say to myself, "If the pebble goes right up to the entrance of the camp it means *very* rich, if it only rolls to the second towel that means *quite* rich, and if it rolls even less than that it means flat broke."

I tried rolling a few pebbles for practice and

they kept getting stuck where the second towel started, until I realized there was a big stumpy bit of tree root sticking up just there, so I started rolling in a different direction.

At three-thirty it started to rain. The sheets got more and more sopping wet and flopped heavily, scraping and flapping on leaves and twigs and getting dirtier and dirtier. The bottom of my trousers began to feel uncomfortably damp too.

Jammy stayed outside the camp even when it was pouring down because Shane, the boss, reckoned that that was Jammy's rightful place. As business manager, Shane was allowed to go home. He said he had some phonecalls to make and some letters to write but Jammy and I think he just wanted to keep out of the wet.

It was five o'clock when Jammy and I decided it was pointless waiting any longer. After all, people don't usually get their fortunes read in the middle of a wood when it's pouring with rain.

We were just about to go when who should turn up but Lisa Farrant!

"Hi, Jammy," she said, with one of her big smiles. "So this is where it all happens, eh? What are you doing?"

I heard Jammy mumble something about a camp, and blow me if he didn't invite her in. I can tell you I felt a real blanko sitting there all dressed up and sparkling. Lisa stared at me for ages, and all the time I got redder and redder even though I concentrated like mad on trying to stop the red coming. I knew I wasn't doing very well because I was getting hotter and hotter.

"So this is the great Signor Psychic Scraggini," she finally said as she crouched down in front of me.

"Get lost, Lisa," I replied. "You're only allowed in here if you're having your fortune told."

"That's what I'm here for," she answered

with another happy little smile that made me really cross.

"You've got to pay, you know," I told her.

She held out her hand with 20p in it.

"Huh!" I said, feeling a bit better now I was in charge more. "It's three pounds fifty, you know."

"Oh, yeah? And how many people have paid that much so far?"

"Well ..."

"Nobody has, have they, Tim? You really haven't got a clue, have you? You should cut your losses and take the 20p." She pushed it under my nose.

Somehow I couldn't bring myself to do the pebble test for Lisa. It's not that she'd laugh or anything, just that there's something about her that makes you feel really stupid when she's anywhere near.

"We're going home now," I told her.

"Okay," she said, without any arguing.

"See you around then. 'Bye, Jammy." And off she went.

Jammy and I didn't mention her all the way home. We walked along kicking pebbles to see whether it would be sunny, wet or cloudy the next day. It came out cloudy.

5

Rubbish

The next day Jammy and I were walking along Leybourne Road when we caught sight of one of our posters poking out of someone's dustbin.

"What a cheek!" I said. "They can't have read it properly. I'm going to get it out and stick it back on a lamppost."

"You can't go in their drive," said Jammy. "What if someone sees you?"

"I don't care if they do," I said, secretly hoping that no one would be looking as I nipped through the gate. I heard a window open just as I yanked the poster out.

"Excuse me, young man, but do you know you're trespassing on private property?"

"Sorry," I said. "I'm just putting this rubbish in your bin."

I looked at the upstairs window. The old bag looked very stern. I was just wondering what to say next when Jammy piped up, "We're on a clean-up campaign. We're tidying up all the rubbish we see. In fact, we can even empty your bin for you if you want."

I thought Jammy must have gone stark raving mad. He was really overdoing it, but the lady from the upstairs window beamed and clasped her hands together as though she'd been on her knees praying for the last half hour that two suckers would come along and empty her bin, and now she was just putting in a quick word of thanks.

"Wait there!" she said.

For a minute I thought she was going to

jump out of the window, but I'd hardly finished telling Jammy what a blanko he was when she rushed out of the front door and came smiling up to the bin. Her hands were still praying.

"Could you *really* empty the bin for me? It's three weeks now since the men have been on strike. Here's 50p for each of you, and I think I could rustle up a couple more for next week — if the strike isn't over, of course."

I stared at the coin in my hand and thought about Fate. It was Fate that made me discover I'm psychic, which made us make posters and stick them up on lampposts, which made this old bird rip one down and stuff it in her bin, which made me pull it out and get caught, which made Jammy invent the clean-up campaign which made us start to get rich. Good old Fate!

The dustbin was on wheels and we pushed and pulled it alternately all the way to the general tip up Creak Hill. As we went I made

up a song and taught it to Jammy. I tried it
with a French accent but it didn't sound much
good so I stuck to American. It went like this:

Creaks and groans and hollers and moans,
Pushing bins up hills, yeah!
Aching joints and muscles and bones,
Don't want rubbish spills, yeah!
We don't want rubbish on the road,
Don't want to lose our rubbishy load,
We've earned a pound and a pound we're
    owed,
So creak creak holler and groan, UGH!

On the UGH! we emptied the bin out on to
the tip, then we whizzed down the hill again,
pushing the empty bin helter skelter all the
way back to the old bird's house. We stood
there puffing and panting and feeling pretty
pleased about the money, especially as lazy
Shane hadn't earned a penny, so we decided
to do another bin as well.

Next door's bin was really bulging. It was

metal with a handle on each side. We both grabbed a handle and lugged it out of the drive without anyone noticing. We did scout's pace all the way to the tip, singing the song loudly as we went.

Why am I always looking or sounding a total blanko when Lisa Farrant suddenly appears?

"Hi, Jammy! Hello, Tim! Good song – catchy lyrics," she commented.

I couldn't tell if she was being sarcastic.

"Tim made it up," piped up Big Mouth.

"Want some help?" Lisa offered.

"Yes," and "No," said Jammy and I at exactly the same moment.

"Don't be stupid," I whispered urgently to Jammy. "That'll be less money for us, and anyway, what if Shane finds out?"

That's when I learnt that Lisa Farrant has not only got big eyes, but big ears as well.

"I'll just help you," she said. "I don't want any money."

Jammy hesitated.

"And Shane doesn't control you, does he, Tim?"

That did it.

"Course not. You can help if you want," I told her, but I knew it wasn't going to be the same with *her* around.

"Okay, teach us the song then, Tim," Lisa immediately said, grabbing the bin from Jammy. "I'll take turns on this side with Jammy," she added.

Jammy started doing that shuffling thing with his feet until I said, "Yeah, okay", then he obviously relaxed.

It was a bit embarrassing at first teaching the song to Lisa, but she didn't take the mickey once, and she learned it really fast. By the time we'd got to the top of the hill I felt as though I'd known her for ages. I even thought she was quite nice but I wasn't going to tell Jammy that, and no way Shane. She ran on down the hill ahead of us because she said she had to be getting back.

The journey back down wasn't such good fun as the last one but it didn't matter because we were still feeling really buzzy.

There was a tissue box amongst the rubbish and I'd ripped a bit off it when we were at the tip. I found a red felt tip pen in my pocket which we'd used for blood when we'd been playing riots one day. I wrote on the card-board in big red letters: HOPE IT'S *BIN* WORTH IT. I wedged the message inside the dustbin lid, facing the house, then Jammy and I shook hands and swore to keep the bin-emptying idea to ourselves and never tell Shane.

"See you tomorrow, Jammy, and not a word to Shane the Pain."

"See you tomorrow, Tim, and hope it doesn't rain again!"

Song writers, bin boys, poets. What a team!

* * *

"Wherever have you been, Tim? I've been worried sick. It's nearly seven o'clock. It's practically dark."

"Sorry, Mum, I lost track of the time. Jammy and me've been emptying people's rubbish for them because of the dustmen's strike."

I decided not to spoil our good deed for the day by telling Mum that we'd earned 50p each.

"Well, that's very laudable, Tim."

"Oh, Mum, I thought you'd be pleased."

"I am. Laudable means praiseworthy." She smiled and said, "Sit down, I've kept your supper warm. What did you think of Bear Nar?" she asked, as she ladled out some very thick soup (or it could have been very thin stew) into my bowl.

"All right, I suppose. Is that a tan he's got, or does he always look like that? I mean, has he been on holiday? Is he going to stay with us?"

Mum laughed and stirred her coffee so

hard it slopped into her saucer. I noticed she'd got blue stuff on her eyes.

"One question at once. Yes, he *has* been on holiday; he's just come back from Normandy actually – a seaside resort quite close to Bayeux, you know, where they've got the Bayeux tapestry about the Norman Conquest.

Mum was beginning to sound like a history teacher so I interrupted her before she decided to give me a test or something.

"Yes, but is he going to stay with us?"

"Yes, he is. He's moving in a week on Monday ready for the new term on the Wednesday."

As well as scoffing Easter eggs, I spent the rest of the holiday with Jammy, emptying bins like it was going out of fashion. We stuck our "Hope it's BIN worth it" note on every bin, and quite frankly it wasn't worth it. Two pounds forty between the two of us was more like slave labour. There are thirty-nine houses on Leybourne Road and we emptied every single bin. On about the fourth bin we saw Shane coming along Dogmere Road as we were crossing over it, so we had to race up the hill to avoid him.

We sat by the tip panting for about five minutes before we had enough breath for the return journey. We didn't want Shane to know what we were doing, in case he tried to drag us back to that soggy Kick Camp, or worse still, tried to set up as business manager and take a cut from the bin job. But we didn't catch sight of Shane *or* Lisa at all after that, and I felt slightly worried about having to see Shane at school, Jammy reckoned he would be feeling pretty bruesome (angry enough for a fight) when he discovered me and Jammy had deserted the Kick Camp and moved on to greener pastures!

Avoiding Shane had made us give strong consideration to being fugitives, but we thought we'd stick to being dustmen while the money was rolling in, not that anything much *did* roll in.

The weather was nice and sunny every single day, which was good for emptying bins but not what the pebbles had forecast, so I decided to blimp being a psychic while I was a dustman.

Then there was Mum to consider. She was behaving rather strangely these days, which made me wonder about being an adult psychologist. Our form teacher said it was jolly useful to have something to fall back on, and with all my career possibilities, I could quite see what he meant.

6

Tampering with the Unknown

On the first day of the summer term Mum and I had breakfast together. The Bear was out jogging. I called him "Bear" to his face once by mistake but he didn't mind a bit so the "Nar" bit got dropped. Even Mum just said Bear now. I was talking about him to Mum that first morning of term.

"Bear's quite an appropriate name for him really, because his chest is very hairy and so is his back. Have a look when he comes in from jogging."

"Honestly, Tim, you shouldn't say such

personal things about people you scarcely know." At that moment the Bear walked in.

"Morning Timotee, Marrrrrg."

"Oh, morning, Bear. Good jog?" Mum was thrusting toast under the grill and desperately squashing three Shredded Wheat into a titchy bowl.

"Wonderful, thank you. Such a beautiful morning. You also must run with me one morning, Timotee?" He made me sound like a well known brand of shampoo.

When he'd gone to have a shower as he called it (although how he managed a shower in our bath I'll never know) I said to Mum, "Why can't he just say Tim like everyone else?"

"He's probably just being considerate, waiting till you invite him to shorten your name."

He came back into the kitchen about five minutes later, stinking of aftershave and deodorant, and Mum nearly dropped the jug of orange juice she was carrying. It was becoming fairly obvious that Mum thought our lodger was all right; and in his dark blue suit and pale blue shirt, I knew he was going to impress all the girls at Maverleys.

Shane wasn't in the same class as Jammy and me and I didn't spot him until Assembly. I kept my eyes glued to my hymn book then had a subtle glance round during the prayer. It looked like most of the school was having a subtle glance round too.

Shane was the first person I saw. He was looking straight at me. I think he was trying to catch my attention, because he was nodding and pointing at me, grinning away and doing something with his hands. He looked as though he was pretending to lift something up. I hoped it wasn't a mime about emptying bins. Funny though – he didn't look at all bruesome.

I glanced at the head teacher up on the

stage. She was glaring at Shane and her prayer was sounding crosser and crosser as though she was telling Shane off but she'd got her wires crossed and God was coming in for an earful.

I frowned hard at Shane and jerked my head in the direction of Mrs Williams, the head teacher. Shane, who can be amazingly thick at times, obviously didn't grasp what I was getting at, because he carried on miming at me vigorously as though he was auditioning for that TV programme *Give Us a Clue*. He pointed to his watch then held up both hands followed by his thumb. I think he was trying to say eleven. Yes, he wanted to talk to me at eleven o'clock (morning break) about lifting something.

Mrs Williams got the whole message. Her prayer was sounding more and more unusual. "Oh God, help us to face up to our problems and make us face the front. Amen."

All the teachers seemed to have coughs that

morning, but when the coughing and the announcements were finished, Mrs Williams said she would like to see Timothy Scragg and Shane Plant in her office straight after Assembly. I rolled my eyes at Shane for being such a blanko, but he was looking completely baffled. I don't think he'd realized he was doing anything wrong.

We wandered down the corridor together, me thinking what a bad start to the new term and Shane prattling on as though there was no problem.

"How did the fortune-telling go? How much money did you earn? I've been dying to find out."

I wasn't prepared for such a pleasant enquiry so I had to think quickly.

"Oh, we had to forget it because Jammy went on holiday and I couldn't do it properly without the doorman."

"We went on holiday too," said Shane. "It was great but I was still glad to get back because I wanted to get on with being your business manager. That's what I was on about in prayers – I think you ought to forget the stupid Kick Camp and try levitation. You'd be good at that."

At that point Mrs Williams opened her office door and stood looking at us with her arms folded and her head on one side.

"I don't recollect hearing anybody knock," she said.

"Sorry," I said, "we were just about to."

"I see," she replied. "Come in." She sat down at her desk and clasped her hands together with the two index fingers sticking out in front as though she was about to shoot us.

"Will one of you explain what all that performance in Assembly was about, please?"

Shane launched in quite happily.

"Well, you see Mrs Williams, we've made an exciting discovery during the holidays. Tim is psychic and I couldn't wait to ask him how much money ..." Shane paused and looked a bit embarrassed. It was bad enough miming all through the prayer but Mrs Williams was going to be even madder if the mime turned out to be a money-spinner. I tried to help Shane out.

"He wanted to talk to me about trying to contact his dead grandfather at a seance, miss."

Mrs Williams turned to Shane.

"Is that right, Shane?"

Shane looked a bit gormless, then his face lit up and I regretted mentioning the seance because I knew what I was letting myself in for.

"Yes, miss," said Shane.

Mrs Williams turned to me.

"And was it Shane's excellent mime or your own psychic powers that enabled you to decode the message, Tim?"

"It's because he's psychic," Shane burst in triumphantly.

Mrs Williams let out a really slow breath and tried to hide a smile like grown-ups often do when they find children amusing. It made me really mad, but blow me, no sooner had she done that stupid smiley face than she suddenly changed and looked really stern.

"The seance is *out*. Do you understand? You do *not* tamper with the unknown." Then, blow me down again if she didn't go all soft-faced.

"And Tim, I shall look forward to seeing some excellent work from you this term. Your new-found skill should prove a great asset to your studies, I would have thought."

Shane nodded enthusiastically. What a blanko!

"Gather round, gather round," said Shane, who was perched up on Jammy's bird bath because it was the only high thing in Jammy's garden. He was addressing all the kids – loads of them — who had followed us there after school.

"Right everybody, we're going to have a serious levitation now. Tim's psychic —"

"What's that?" someone called out.

"Seeing into the future," Shane answered hurriedly. "We discovered it in the holidays. Now Tim, tell us what to do," he ordered.

A serious levitation! I hadn't the foggiest idea what a levitation was. I thought it involved lifting up someone who was lying on the floor, only using one finger. It sounded really dangerous. I mean, you could break your finger, couldn't you? Oh, borgonzola! It looked like I was going to be responsible for a load of broken fingers. How on earth was I going to get out of this one without looking totally blatant?

I looked doubtfully at all the kids standing round waiting for a show. My spirits had sunk so low they were probably somewhere in Australia. And it was at that very moment that

Jammy's mum appeared. She looked round suspiciously. Shane grinned and her eyes went narrow.

"Are you playing vicars up there, Shane, or Julius Caesar or what?"

"Actually, I was making an important announcement about Tim," said Shane.

Yea, bangler! I thought. Go on, Shane, tell her we're about to do a levitation, then she'll say, "You will do no such thing in *my* garden! Be off with you, the lot of you!"

But all she said was, "Well, here's an important announcement about tea, Nicholas. You've got twenty minutes. Okay?"

Jammy nodded and I wished his tea was going to be in two minutes, not twenty.

"Right, Tim," smiled Shane. "You can start now. I'm his business manager," he added, looking round, but he needn't have bothered because nobody was interested in pinching Shane's job as business manager, they just wanted me to do something clever. I don't expect half of them even knew what a levitation was.

I suddenly caught sight of Pushty with his two mates Steve and Foggs. Pushty was in his usual pose, hands on hips, head on one side, looking at me as if to say, "Do it or else!"

I felt sick. In fact I'm sure I would have been sick if Lisa Farrant hadn't popped up at that moment and started talking.

"Tim, you mustn't do it," she said.

She's only small, Lisa, and she's got quite a soft voice as well, but people listen when she talks. Everyone looked at her, then all the heads turned to Pushty.

"Oh, yeah?" he said in a scornful voice. "Trying to get Timmy out of a tight spot are we, Lisa? Because he's too scared to admit that he's got absolutely no psychic powers whatsoever."

Pushty stuck his tongue into his cheek and nodded slowly. Foggs and Steve sneered to show they agreed with Pushty.

"Go on Tim, show him," said Shane, not too loudly.

"Yeah, show him," said one or two brave voices.

"Don't do it, Tim," said Lisa, and Pushty looked daggers at her. "Don't you know anything?" she carried on, looking furiously at Shane. "You mustn't meddle with supernatural forces – you never know what could happen. It's messing about like this in people's back gardens with a load of idiots who don't know what they're doing that stirs ghosts, you know. Why do you think that Tim's always kept it to himself that he's psychic?"

"Because he's not, that's why," sneered Pushty.

"No Pushty, you're wrong," retorted Lisa, and a girl called Mandy dug her in the ribs and whispered, "Shut up, Lisa, Pushty's looking really mad."

But Lisa took no notice and quite a few people began to look worried as she went on.

"You've got to be really thick if you think psychic people can operate in these surroundings," and she spread her hands to show she meant Jammy's garden. "There's no atmosphere and far too many people."

"Okay, clever little Lisa, let's clear the people and choose a better place, then Tim can give us a proper demonstration. Right?"

"Yeah, good idea, Pushty," answered Lisa. Her eyes were glinting and she didn't seem to care at all about Pushty even though her friends were trying to shut her up, and Mandy looked as though she was about to burst into tears. One or two kids had begun to sneak away because they could see trouble brewing. The frightening thing about Pushty – and everybody knows this – is that if you make him cross, he'll save it up, sometimes for ages, and then get you back when you're not expecting it at all.

"Right, let's clear all the people away. I know, we can start with you," went on Lisa. "Go on, Pushty, clear off!"

One of the girls gasped, then there was silence. I could see Pushty's right fist clenching and unclenching. His eyes looked black and cruel. It suddenly came to me that Lisa was doing all this to help *me* and I knew I ought to help *her*, but I had the distinct feeling that the next to speak would get Pushty's fist in their mouth. Shane's face was all white. Jammy shuffled his feet and looked at his watch. Then a voice behind Pushty caught everyone's attention.

"'Scuse me breaking up the party, but you've got to come home, Shane."

It was Shane's brother Douglas. Shane looked dead relieved.

"Yeah. Okay, Doug, just coming," he said, and he practically ran over to his brother, which made Douglas rather suspicious. He looked round and his eyes rested on Pushty.

"What's going on?" he asked.

Somehow Pushty didn't look quite so cool when faced with Douglas, who was six foot two and did weight training at the gym twice a week.

"Don't ask me," answered Pushty.

"What's going on?" repeated Douglas, but this time he was asking Shane. Shane looked down. It was Lisa who spoke.

"Pushty's going on!" she said. "On and on and on!" and she yawned as though Pushty was really boring and wouldn't stop talking. One or two of the girls sniggered because we all felt a bit safer with Douglas around. Douglas smiled what you might call the ghost of a smile, which was quite appropriate because of what Lisa had said about stirring ghosts.

"Well, I reckon it's about your teatime too, isn't it, Jammy?" Douglas asked.

"Just what I was thinking," said Jammy, studying his watch again.

"Yeah, we'd better go too," said Mandy. "Come on, Lisa."

Lisa gave Pushty a triumphant "don't care" look and sauntered off with her friends. The other kids all followed suit. I went and stood by Douglas.

"See you then, Pushty," said Douglas, turning to go.

Pushty answered "Yeah, see ya!" then in a horrible loud voice called out, "See ya, Lisa!"

The girls, who were nearly out of sight, heard him and turned round. One of them clamped her hand on her mouth then grabbed Lisa's arm before they all ran off.

I thought about the whole episode as I stared at the telly that night. I wasn't really watching whatever was on, just having private thoughts without Mum knowing. Bear was in the kitchen marking away. He had this irritating habit of half whispering all that he was reading in the exercise books and as he turned the pages, he flipped them really hard so they made a slapping noise. It got on my nerves but Mum didn't appear to notice.

As I stared at the screen I kept thinking about Lisa and how brave she was. And she was right, I shouldn't let Shane boss me around. I suddenly had an ace thought. Perhaps Lisa could be one of the people at the seance, then she could tell Shane it was all rubbish.

"Yea, bangler!" I said out loud, and Mum jerked her head from the telly to me.

"What?" she said.

"Yea, bangler," I repeated.

"Oh, yes," she said.

Poor Mum. She was always in a dream these days – never heard a thing I said.

"Mum?" I said a moment later, just to test her, "Mum, is it all right if I swing on the ring round Saturn tomorrow?"

"Mm . . . I should think so . . ."

Poor Mum!

*   *   *

"Lisa!" I called out frantically the next morning, spotting her going into the school library. She turned round.

"Umm ... thanks for saying that stuff yesterday."

"I only said it because I believe it," she answered, which made me feel really blatant because I'd assumed she'd said it to help me out. "Anyway, you shouldn't let Shane boss you around like that. And as for Pushty, he needed taking down a peg or two."

Nothing seemed to worry Lisa.

"We're having a seance tonight at Jammy's at six o'clock. Why don't you come?" I asked her as casually as I could.

"Shane bossing you around again, is he?" Lisa asked, tilting her head.

"Oh, no ... it'll be good ... you ought to come." I tried grinning but I could tell she thought I was a bit of a blanko.

"Do you really think it'll be good fun, Tim? Because personally I think it's tampering."

"It doesn't do any harm. It's just for fun," I tried.

"That's just how trouble starts," said Lisa. "Idiots like you mucking around with what you don't understand 'just for fun'! Please Tim, just for me, tell Shane to get stuffed."

Everything was small about Lisa except her eyes. I couldn't stop staring at them. They reminded me of that story *The Tinder Box* — about the dog with eyes as big as saucers. Even when she'd gone into the library her eyes still seemed to be hanging up on the door.

She was right about one thing though; I *would* be mucking about with what I didn't understand because I don't know anything about seances. Shane said I was going to contact dead people with my psychic powers. I wished Shane would drop dead himself. Also, I wished I'd never started that pebble-kicking thing in the first place.

The next day Shane kept on and on about the

seance. The first time he mentioned it was in the dinner queue.

"Great idea of yours, Tim. Can't wait to see who you contact tonight. Dave's grandad died about two months ago and Dave wants to ask him what it's like being dead."

"I'm not sure about all this, Shane," I tried. "I mean, contacting dead people is a bit different from kicking pebbles to see into the future ..."

"No, it's all linked up," said Shane. "It's all to do with your mind. Anyway, if you do it okay tonight, we're going to be really rich. Everyone'll want you to contact their dead relatives. You just wait!"

I was dreading it. I ate hardly any dinner, and I felt as though a big weight was sitting on my head for the rest of the afternoon. Shane wouldn't let me out of his sight. He even walked home with me.

Mum made boiled eggs and soldiers for tea for Shane and me. It was really embarrassing –

she hadn't done soldiers since I was about four. Thank goodness Shane wasn't in a mocking mood. I just wished something would happen to make him forget all about the stupid seance.

"Oh, by the way, Tim," said Mum, "a letter came for you today."

She dropped it by my plate. I opened it and started to read it slowly. Mum was leaning over me reading it too. She kept gasping and saying, "Oh, Tim, that's wonderful!"

Shane kept on saying "What's it say? What's it say?" but Mum and I ignored him till we'd got to the end. Then Mum gave me a big smacking kiss with her hands on my shoulders, as though I was the World Cup and she was the captain of the winning team.

"What's it say?" Shane asked for the tenth time.

"Tim's been chosen to appear on *Jim'll Fix It*, the television show!"

Shane looked gobsmacked.

"Tim's going to be famous," he said slowly with big wide eyes. He jumped up from his chair. "Tim's going on television and *I'm* the first one to know! Thanks for the tea, Mrs Scragg. See you tomorrow, Tim."

He couldn't get out fast enough. He was going to spread it all round town but I didn't care. I was doubly happy. One: Shane had forgotten all about the seance; two: my dream was about to come true.

7

The Bear's Fiancée

The Bear's fiancée turned up on Saturday morning. She was called Janine. She looked really young and trendy. Her hair went down to her waist and was halfway between carrots and brown. When she leaned over me once to correct something in my French homework, that hair hung all over my neck and shoulder. It looked as though it was *my* hair.

She wore weird clothes but acted as if she looked normal and after a bit you found yourself thinking that she did look normal –

well, not quite so weird anyway. She changed her clothes loads of times.

When she came down on Saturday morning I thought she'd forgotten to put her skirt on. Mum must have seen me staring because when I was waiting for the toast to pop up, she stood right next to me, and without moving her lips she hissed, "Don't stare. It's the fashion."

Janine wore five different jumpers even though she only stayed two days. Her smell was so strong I had to have a bath every time she came anywhere near me, in case the smell stuck to me, otherwise Jammy and Shane might have thought I'd been putting perfume on or something.

At about twelve-thirty on Saturday when I went into the kitchen I couldn't see Mum at first because of all the steam.

"Oh, Tim, it's *you*. Thank goodness!" she said as though I'd just emerged from the fog on some distant mountain top where teams of people had been searching for me for weeks.

"Why's it all steamy, Mum?"

"It's the vegetables. I'm doing them fast because Bear and Janine will be back from the pub soon. I told them lunch was at quarter to one. Be a love and lay the table, Tim. Use the white tablecloth from the bottom drawer," she called as I walked into the sitting room where the posh table was.

I opened the drawer and had a real bodger. Uh-oh! No tablecloth. You know where both Mum's best white tablecloths were, don't you? Yeah, the Kick Camp.

I stared into space and used every single cell in my brain for about fifteen seconds, and came up with a bangler. Bear's bedspread was white. Mum would never notice the difference when it was all covered with plates and knives and forks and stuff. I belted upstairs and took it off Bear's bed. It looked funny on the table. It needed covering.

I worked hard for the next five minutes. I carried every single dish of vegetables, the gravy, the mint sauce, the butter, the water jug, the wine bottle – everything through to the sitting room. There was still a bit of bedspread showing right in the middle so I told Mum we ought to have a vase of flowers on the table.

"Lovely idea, Tim, but we haven't got any."

I legged it upstairs and took down the hanging plant from the landing. It looked great in the middle of the table with all the hanging bits wrapped round the bottom. I was only just in time.

"That's right," Mum was saying, with a red shiny face from all the steam, "come in and sit down." She whipped off her apron and ushered Bear and Janine into the sitting room.

Janine was wearing a floppy yellow jumper that came down to her knees and some blue boots that came up to the jumper. Mum was doing a lot of sudden smiles. I could tell she was nervous. So was I, because I'd just realized that the bedspread came right down to the floor on one side of the table and only halfway down on the other side. I quickly sat down at the long side.

"Let Janine sit there, Tim. That's right, next to Bear. You come on this side, then you're handy to help me with clearing and carrying. Well done love, you *have* been a help," she added, as I sat down next to her desperately hoping that Janine would think all English tablecloths came down to the floor on one side.

I didn't enjoy that dinner one bit because of wondering how to get the bedspread back up to Bear's room before he went up there himself. Mum and Janine were trying to have a conversation. Mum doesn't speak French and Janine speaks hardly any English so as you can imagine, it was a pretty quiet conversation. It was all about clothes and how much they cost in France compared to England. They kept pointing at each other's clothes and smiling and nodding. Bear was filling up their wine glasses every time they were empty. He must have had a supply of French wine in the hall because twice he went out and came back with another bottle. All in all the grown-ups got through quite a lot of wine.

The French for "how much" is "combien". Even I knew that from my French lessons. Mum said "combianne?" with a stupid little laugh as she pointed to Janine's jumper. Then Janine pointed to Mum's skirt and said "Ow murch?" Bear smiled at me, rolling his eyes to the ceiling as if to say "Women!" Then Mum pointed to her own shoe and raised her eyebrows, showing Janine she wanted to know combianne her boots cost.

Janine kicked her right leg up in the air. A bedspread tassel had got caught in the buckle of her boot, and the next thing I knew the whole bedspread shifted sideways and the gravy toppled on to the floor followed by Bear's wine glass, which hit the bottle he'd got stashed under the table, and smashed into pieces as it sprayed red wine everywhere.

Mum was saying, "Not to worry," with eyes like daggers, making it quite clear that *she* was certainly worried. Bear got up a bit too fast and knocked into the table sending Mum's wine glass flying, and Mum still said, "Not to worry," through tight lips.

Suddenly she put her hands on her hips and marched round to Janine's side of the table. There she stood like a teacher, staring accusingly at the spattered bedspread which by this time was draping on the carpet.

"I see," she said in a high voice.

I just sat there. I felt as though I was stuck to my chair. Bear opened a bottle of white wine, got a cloth and started pouring it all over the red wine stains and rubbing away.

"Whatever —?" spluttered Mum.

"Zee action of zee white wine on zee red is verrry gooood."

But Mum wasn't listening, she was just spluttering and panicking. "B-b-but w-w-what ..."

Janine had obviously picked up Mum's little phrase from earlier on. She put her arm round Mum and guided her to a chair saying, "Nut to wurrrrrry," as she patted Mum's shoulder. "Bear is man intelligent."

She made it sound as though Bear was the first of his species, like Homo Sapiens. I could hear Mum muttering to herself as Janine rushed back to help Bear clear up.

"He might be the most intelligent man on God's earth but that won't clear up this mess."

When all the dishes and plates and everything had been taken into the kitchen, I quickly grabbed the bedspread and shoved it into the washing machine.

"Mum, how do you work this washing

machine?" I asked her, trying to sound helpful. She didn't answer, just took hold of my wrist and marched me upstairs. We stood together in Bear's room staring at the bed.

"Whatever possessed you to use a bedspread for a tablecloth, Tim?" she asked without looking at me.

"Because the other one wasn't there and I thought you'd be cross."

"And where *is* the other one, Tim?"

"Um ... it's ... at school. We're talking about Irish linen in geography and we had to take examples in to show ..."

"Make sure that tablecloth is back here on Monday, and now go and explain to Bear why his bedspread has been adorning our dining table, please. Go on! Get *on* with it!"

She was really mad. I raced downstairs, called out, "Sorry about your bedspread, Bear. It's in the wash. Got to go now, sorry." Then I rushed to Kennel Woods as fast as I could.

Twenty minutes later I was on Shane's doorstep clutching Mum's tablecloths and hoping two things: one, that Shane would answer the door; and two, that Shane knew how to operate his mum's washing machine.

The tablecloths were revolting – all heavy and slimy brown. My first prayer wasn't answered. Mrs Plant came to the door.

"Hello, Tim," she said with a big grin. "Come in, love. What have you got there?"

"I was wondering if I could wash these please, Mrs Plant. Our washing machine's broken down."

"Be my guest," she said, taking the two dirty sodden tablecloths from me and loading them into her washing machine. They'd dripped brown water all over the floor, but she didn't mind, just got one of those floor mops and mopped it up. She's not like a mother, Shane's mum isn't. She doesn't get cross about the usual things that make mothers cross. Shane walked in at that moment.

"Wotcher, Tim!"

"Hi!"

"Tim's washing machine has broken down. I'm just washing his . . . What *is* it I'm washing exactly, Tim?"

"Tablecloths – they fell on to the soil from the washing line and got left out all night you see," I said, going a bit red.

Mrs Plant ruffled my hair, giggled a bit and told me I was a right one.

Nobody said any more about the bedspread that day or the next. I stayed out of the house as much as possible and by Sunday evening when it was time for Janine to go, everyone seemed to be calm and friendly again.

The only trouble with French people being friendly is all the kissing. Janine gave me four kisses – two on either cheek – at least five times during that weekend. "Ah, Bibiche!"

she would say, then all the hair would come swooping down on me. The kissing got worse the better she knew us, and by the time she was going I counted five kisses a session between her and mum. I'm surprised more French people haven't got broken noses, they swop sides so fast. Bear took Janine to the airport, which was a shame because Shane said I might get the chance to see some proper French kissing before she went.

While they were going to the airport I had a bath, partly to get rid of the perfumy smell and partly to keep out of Mum's way. It was going to take her a little while to get over the tablecloth incident.

8

Skiving

The next few days seemed rather quiet. I was marking off the days until the *Jim'll Fix It* day. There were thirty-four to go. I wanted to buy some new clothes but Mum said leave it till nearer the time because it might be really hot by then and I'd need summer clothes. But all the time I wasn't allowed new clothes, Mum was buying shopfuls.

First I noticed her new jeans, then a new blue shirt which made her look like an American footballer. And the next day ...

"What do you think then, Tim?"

What did I think? Borgonzola, she *was* turning posh! A black and white jacket like the top of a suit.

"What are those bits stuck on your legs, Mum?"

"They are not bits, and they are not stuck on my legs. It's the pattern on the tights."

She started twisting and turning and flicking her hair about.

"Is it all new?" I asked.

"Yes. Like it?" She was in a really good mood these days, spinning and smiling all over the place.

"It looks expensive," I said.

"Oh, good," she said. "That shows it's quality."

When she said that I felt my tea going up and down in my stomach.

"Going to do my homework," I mumbled, and went upstairs.

I lay on the bed feeling really brinked

(totally sad). It was obvious what Mum was up to – shoplifting. Yes, I know you're thinking, Hang on a sec, Tim, you were wrong last time, but this time there was no doubt about it. She couldn't possibly afford all that gear. She'd started part-time work in the bookshop and she'd got Bear's lodging money, but I was sure that wasn't enough to pay for so many new clothes.

"Tim," she called out about ten minutes later, "come and look at this. Jimmy Saville's on one of those chat shows."

I couldn't watch because my eyes kept going back to what Mum had got hanging round her neck. It looked like gold. I felt sick.

"Mum, is that *real* gold, that necklace?"

She fingered it as though it was a treasured family heirloom.

"No," she said with a little laugh. "I wish it was! And look, I've got these to match."

She pushed her hair behind her ears and I could see glistening gold earrings dangling down almost as far as her shoulders. I thought of going round to Pat's to see if she could talk some sense into Mum, but I didn't want Mum feeling stupid, so I decided to keep a careful eye on her for a while, though that would be difficult when I was at school all day.

I knew Mum would be working in the bookshop on Mondays, Wednesday mornings, Thursdays and Fridays. On Wednesday afternoons most shops were closed so the most likely day for her to try anything would be Tuesday. I needed to find a way of keeping her indoors especially on Tuesdays so she couldn't go out stealing. There was a word for people like Mum – clapometers or something. The word clapometer suddenly made me remember this programme on computers we watch at school on Tuesday afternoons, and *that* gave me a great bangler.

"Mum, could you tape this programme for me on Tuesday? It's called Computer Maniacs."

"Course I can. It must be good if you want to watch it at school *and* home. What time does it start and finish?"

"Quarter to three till half past," I said, congratulating myself that I'd thought of such a bangling way to keep her in, right in the middle of the afternoon.

"Okay, love, I'll preset it."

"Preset it? Why?" I hadn't thought of that.

"Well, I usually go out on Tuesdays."

"Do you? Where?"

"Oh ... into town ... just places ... you know."

I slid back down in the chair as far as I could. My chin rested on my chest and I folded my arms.

"Don't scowl, Tim," she said. "It doesn't suit you."

Tuesday afternoons were double English and music – quite a difficult afternoon to skive but it had to be done. English was my best subject.

The English teacher, Mrs Rawlinson, always gave me good marks and a great report, and she put decent comments on my exercise book too. One parents' evening she told Mum that I produced extremely imaginative writing, and if I could only work on spellings and things I'd be one of the best in the class. Whenever we had discussion in English lessons, Mrs Rawlinson chose me when nobody put their hand up.

"Tim, any ideas?" she always said, and I usually had quite a few.

It was going to be tricky. She was sure to ask where I was. Same with old Rigid Bottom.

"Where's your big voice, Tim?" she always said in singing lessons, beaming like billy-o and playing the piano louder than ever.

I decided to tell Jammy my plan so he could tell Mrs Rawlinson and Rigid Bottom where I was.

"Say I've gone to the dentist, okay?"

"Yeah, but where are you going really?"

"Nowhere much; I just fancied having the afternoon off," I said casually.

"Bet you're going to meet a girl somewhere," jeered Jammy, with his silly face grinning at me from about ten centimetres away.

"Okay, if you *must* know, I'm going to meet Ricky Stone."

"Ricky Stone!" Jammy sneered. "Huh! Belief!" he said sarcastically.

I'd done it again. Said something stupid without thinking. Ricky Stone was the lead singer of the group Treadmill. There was no going back. I'd said it and I had to carry on with that stupid story.

"No, honestly. He used to know my dad really well, and he still comes to see Mum occasionally."

"Cor, Ricky Stone! Borgonzola! Get us his autograph."

"Yeah, yeah, okay, but don't tell anyone."

"Why not? I thought you'd want everyone to know."

"No, because he told me not to tell anyone. He's just coming to see me and Mum, see?"

"D'you miss your dad, Tim?"

"Not really. I was only three when he died, so I can't remember him much, you see."

After lunch I nipped out of school. I didn't think anybody had seen me and I began to feel quite buzzy, except when the bodger about Ricky Stone came into my head. Eventually even Jammy's brain would work out that being friends with Ricky Stone would have been my passport to loads of concerts and tickets for TV shows and things. I'd never been to a concert in my life.

I didn't want to risk dropping my satchel off at home in case Mum was still there, so I stuffed it between two fat fir trees outside someone's house in Fenton Lane. The trees hid it so well I decided to stuff my anorak in there as well, then I made my way down to the town centre, keeping a careful watch all around me. When I was just passing the post office I saw Foggs' mum posting a letter. If she saw me she might tell Foggs and Foggs would tell Pushty and that would spell big trouble.

I turned and ran all the way home as fast as I could. Mum was definitely out because the toilet window was shut. I grabbed the spare key from the hole under the windowsill and went in. Ten minutes later I came out again, clicked the door shut, locked it with the spare key, put the key back in its hole and set off.

My disguise wasn't much good but it was all I could manage – a pair of very black sunglasses and my hair sticking up on end with Mum's hair gel. I also found a very nice brown leather jacket hanging up with our other coats and jackets. It must have been Bear's because it was far too big for Mum. Too big for me, too. It went right down to my knees and the sleeves were twice as long as my arms but I rolled and bunched them up till my hands showed, then gripped the cuffs hard to stop them sliding off again.

I went into Marks and Spencer's first, but no sign of Mum at all. I tried four more big shops without any luck and was just about to turn round and go home when I saw her through the window of a shop called Shoe-string and Glitter. It was a medium-sized shop full of clothes and handbags and necklaces and things. Mum was flicking through a rail of dresses. She was smiling and talking to someone but it was impossible to see who, without pressing right up against the window which might have given the game away. I waited till she moved to the other end of the shop then sneaked in and pretended to look at some earrings.

"Can I help you?" a sales assistant asked me, and Mum chose that very moment to walk briskly out. I stared intently at the earrings and mumbled "No, thank you," then sidled out of the shop with my head down, feeling really blatant. I looked up as soon as I dared and spotted Mum going into Debenhams, so I decided to follow her. When I'd given her a bit of a start I swung the door open and who should I bash straight into but Lisa! I was hoping that she wouldn't recognize me but there was no chance of that.

"Tim! Oh, my God, Tim!" she squealed, clapping her hand over her mouth. At that moment I wished that a hole in the ground would appear and gobble me up.

It seemed like about three years before Lisa spoke again. Her eyes were even bigger than usual as she stared at me in my cool gear that suddenly felt totally blatant. I was on the point of telling her that I was going to a fancy dress party when she spluttered, "And don't tell me you're going to a fancy dress party – I'd never believe you."

With that she clutched her stomach and fell

about laughing while I just stood there like a blanko, then she suddenly grabbed me and pulled me into Debenham's.

I tottered behind her for about fifty metres of ground floor make-up and perfume, jewellery, gloves, stockings and handbags. Then she dragged me up the escalator and round the corner. Next she frogmarched me through thousands of dresses, skirts, jackets, trousers and separates (whatever they were), and finally pushed me into a teeny little L-shaped corner on the first floor where there was just room for the two of us. There she yanked off my sunglasses and stuffed them in her pocket, ordered me to take off the jacket, and whipped out a brush and began flattening my hair down.

As she worked on me she said, "Anyway, what's it in aid of, this dressing-up business? The truth, please."

I suddenly felt cross.

"What's it to you anyway?" I snapped at her.

Most girls would have sneered or sulked but not Lisa. She just kept her eyes on mine and said, "Come on. Spill."

I wanted to tell her. I reckoned Lisa would probably know the best thing to do about Mum and the shoplifting, and I was about to explain everything when Mum's head, followed by the rest of her body, suddenly came into view at the top of the escalator.

"I can't talk here," I said, trying to sound mysterious and hoping she might think I belonged to MI5 or some other organization like that.

"Okay. Come on. My place," she said.

We talked all the way to her house, but not about Mum or anything. It made me like Lisa more because she didn't go on and on trying to get me to tell her what I'd been doing in town. Instead I told her about the pebbles and we tried it but it didn't work. She laughed and said it was good fun, but rubbish really. Then I told her about the B Club and all the words beginning with B. She said, "I know, let's make up a song using all the words beginning with B." So we did and we marched along singing it. This is how it went. You sing it to the tune of The Grand Old Duke of York.

Oh, the blatant Duke of York!
He buzzed about all day,
He sang some bandy songs but then
A bodger came his way.
He said I'm feeling brinked,
I hate my bruesome brain,
But then a bangler blimped the bodge
And he buzzed about again.

Just as we got to the end of the song, who should appear from Wilbury Avenue but Pushty! I grabbed Lisa's arm.

"Quick! Run before Pushty sees us," I said,

beginning to break into a run, but Lisa pulled me back.

"We're perfectly entitled to be walking along the road together. School will have finished by now. Just ignore him."

"Hi, Tim! How's your girlfriend?" came Pushty's horrible voice.

Lisa calmly turned round and said, "I'm very well, thank you, Pushty, but please don't be too scared to ask me yourself the next time – I won't bite, you know."

I could see Pushty's face go all ugly. Lisa would be for it now, and probably me too. She carried on singing as though nothing had happened and I joined in too, but I can't say that I enjoyed it. Pushty disappeared.

Lisa's kitchen was very yellow and shiny. There were about twenty plants standing or hanging all over the place. As soon as we walked through the door she started watering them all. She talked to them as she was watering. She didn't care that I was listening.

"Where's your mum?" I asked her.

"Staying with my aunt," she said. "Auntie Alice. She's having a breakdown and Mum's looking after her till Friday."

"Where's your dad then?"

"At work. He'll be back at six-thirty."

"What were you doing in town?" I asked.

"I had the afternoon off – to see Mum off, you know."

Lisa set the table properly and made tea and put out biscuits. She offered me one.

"So, what were *you* doing, Tim?"

"Spying on Mum."

"No kidding. Why?"

"She's got all these new clothes and I knew she could never afford them, so I wondered if she ... if she was ..."

"If she was stealing?" asked Lisa quietly.

"Yeah," I said.

"You went to a lot of trouble – the disguise and everything."

"I didn't want anyone to recognize me."

"In case it got back to a teacher?"

"Or someone like ... Jammy." Half of me wished I hadn't said that.

"Doesn't Jammy know, then?"

"He thinks I'm meeting my old friend ... Ricky."

Lisa was looking at me without anything in her eyes – no look of curiosity, no look of disbelief, just big eyes, waiting.

"Well actually," I tried again, "he thinks I'm meeting Ricky Stone."

I watched her, expecting to see a big grin starting, but she just looked a bit puzzled and I realized she'd never heard of Ricky Stone.

"You know, the pop star – he plays with the group Treadmill," I explained.

"I expect Jammy'll forget you said that. I should tell him he must be going deaf if he mentions it again. Say you never said *anything* about Ricky Stone. It's more important to worry about your mum than that. You might be right. She might be stealing. But you might be totally wrong, you never know," she said thoughtfully. Then the phone rang. It made me jump.

"Hi," said Lisa into the mouthpiece. "Yeah, fine. Yeah, don't worry . . . I'm having tea with a boy called Tim from school. How's Auntie Alice? Did you give her my cushion? Did you tell her how long it took me? Yeah . . . Lots of love to Auntie Alice . . . and you. See you Friday. Okay, I'll tell Dad. Yeah, he said he's phoning tonight . . . Okay, I'll tell him. Bye, Mum. See you Friday . . . Bye."

She put the phone down and came back to the table. Lisa never pretends to be anything she isn't. I wished I dared to be like that in front of other people.

A bit later as I was going out of the door she said, "Tim, why not go back to Jammy and say he must have misheard you because you said Ricky *Stern* not Ricky *Stone*."

"The only trouble is, he knows I was talking about someone famous because he went on about autographs."

"Well, it's up to you but I reckon it's Ricky Stern or the truth."

I ran back to Fenton Lane, picked up my satchel and anorak, put the anorak on, then walked home slowly thinking about the truth. When I got home Mum was cooking. She was wearing a new jumper. It was very thin and not woolly like an ordinary jumper. It looked expensive. She'd got a black and red scarf draped round her shoulders and she'd had her hair done. On the dresser I noticed a new black handbag. I could hardly speak, I was so brinked. I knew what I must do.

9

Mr Stern

After school on Thursday I belted straight down to Debenhams on an important mission. It was a safe bet that Mum would be at the bookshop.

I walked round Debenham's like a detective, spotting all Mum's clothes, the handbag, the earrings, the necklace, even the tights. It took me ages to find everything but it was all there. Every single new thing Mum had got (except the jeans, because there were so many pairs it was impossible to tell) had come from

Debenham's. I reckoned she'd spent over two hundred pounds in there, Borgonzola!

The next thing I had to do was the most important bit of the mission. I went home, got a big bag from the kitchen cupboard, then went up to Mum's room and carefully put all the new clothes, the jewellery and the hand-bag inside. It was going to be absolutely awful when she discovered it was gone, but for once I was doing the right thing taking it all back. At least Mum would never be found out. It was what you called being cruel to be kind. Lisa had suggested I talk to Mum about it, but I reckoned this was a much better idea, and I was sure Lisa would be proud of me when she knew what I'd done.

I felt nervous in Debenham's. My heart was really beating. I decided to have a quick look on every floor just to check Mum wasn't at it again. When I got to the first floor something propelled me towards that little L-shaped place where Lisa had got me out of my disguise. There in the corner on the floor, where no one would dream of looking, was that brown jacket. I thought I'd better take it home before Bear missed it, so I put it on and rolled the sleeves right up, then nipped down to the ground floor so that I could put the earrings and necklace back first.

I spent ages standing by the necklaces pretending to choose one. Mum's necklace was in my hand but I dithered and dithered before putting it on the little rail with the others. I was feeling really strange and guilty doing all this shoplifting in reverse.

Eventually I hooked the necklace into place and then looked round to check no one had seen me before getting the earrings out. All the other earrings were on little pads and I wasn't sure how to put Mum's ones back. I mean, I couldn't really just leave them on their own with no little pad. Then I noticed that one of the pads hadn't got anything on it. That must have been Fate giving me a hand. I looked round carefully. No one was looking so I carefully fixed on one of the earrings then nearly jumped out of my skin as a man's voice behind me said, "Could I take a look in that bag, please?"

BORGONZOLA!

I turned round and looked at him. He was tall and thin with piercing eyes and big ears. He was bending down. I had dropped the other earring back into my bag by mistake. The man found it. It rested on his flat palm. His cold eyes were on me.

"No need to look further, is there? I know what I'm going to find."

He sucked in his cheeks and took a slow breath as he pulled out all Mum's clothes one by one. I stood there, all brinked and blatant while loads of shoppers slowed down to have a good stare. There was suddenly an enormous amount of interest in Debenham's necklaces at that moment.

"Bit young to have a lady friend, aren't you?"

"They're ... they're ... Mum's ..." I managed to whisper a bit hoarsely.

"Shopping for Mum, eh?" the man said.

"No, I'm putting it back for Mum," I told him.

"Well, I've heard a good many stories in my time, but I reckon this one takes the biscuit."

He stuffed everything back in the bag and pushed me in front of him.

"Up four floors, sonny. We'll see what the manager has to say."

My legs felt so heavy I could hardly walk. Nobody would ever believe I was putting the stuff back. I felt glummer and glummer. I was trapped in a corner and wondered what Lisa would do, then I realized that Lisa would never have got herself in such a fix in the first place. We were on the fourth floor. The man was knocking on a door. On the door in gold letters it said, R STERN.

"Come in," someone called.

As we walked in I was certain I was dreaming. The room was posh and comfortable at the same time. A big man was sitting in a black armchair. He stood up when we went in, and said to the lady who was sitting in the other armchair, "Excuse me, please, while I deal with this little problem."

My eyes nearly popped out of my head while my feet took root in the ground when I saw who it was. She spoke in a weak little voice, "Tim!"

I answered with a strange throaty noise, "Mmmum!"

The next three seconds took three years to go by. At least that's what it felt like. Mr Stern's face was looking as though it wasn't sure what expression to wear. It went from anxious to surprised to horrified to panicky, back to anxious and finally settled on confused. I know it did all those things because I watched him all the time.

"You obviously ... know this boy, Margery?" he asked Mum hesitantly.

"This is Tim, the one and only," said Mum, looking at the ceiling.

Mr Stern's face relaxed. He patted Mum's hand and sat down.

"Right, thank you," he said to the tall thin man who'd brought me to see him. "I think we can take it from here."

"Stealing earrings at the time I noticed him, Mr Stern," said the man. "You'll see for yourself though that that isn't all. Been crafty enough to remove the labels from the stuff in the bag, but it's very obviously brand new ..."

"Yes, thank you, Reg, I'm in the picture now," said Mr Stern.

While the man had been telling Mr Stern all that, Mum had gradually slumped forward, resting her forehead on her hand. Her eyes were closed. I think she was probably wishing for a hole to appear in the ground. So Reg went out and Mr Stern turned to me.

"Tim," he said, "you've caused your mother an awful lot of worry. We're both hoping there is a perfectly reasonable expla-nation for what appears to be shoplifting."

As he was talking he was pulling Mum's things out of the bag, and a look of confusion was beginning to spread over his face.

"Wait a minute," Mum suddenly said, springing to life, "this is that handbag you bought me, and here's the necklace . . . and my skirt, my shirt . . . my jacket . . . it's all here. Tim." She suddenly stood up very straight. "Tim, tell Mr Stern *exactly* what you are doing with my clothes."

"Putting them back because I thought you stole them."

There was another three years' silence and then Mum flopped back in the chair as though she was exhausted.

"Well," she finally said to Mr Stern, "I told you it was difficult to fathom the way Tim's brain works, didn't I?"

And they both cracked up laughing. Mum put her arm round my shoulder and said, "We've got a lot of talking to do, Tim. Come on."

She guided me to the door and looked back at Mr Stern. "We'll see you later."

We were nearly out of the door when Mr Stern suddenly called out, "Hey, wait a minute – he's wearing my jacket!"

"I thought it was Bear's," I said, looking at Mum.

She went pink.

"As I said, Tim, we've got a lot of talking to do."

On the evening of that same day we were sitting in the garden of the Ewe and Lamb – me, Mr Stern and Mum in her earrings and necklace.

To cut a long story short, it turned out that Mr Stern, who was the Manager of Debenhams, was also Mum's new boyfriend. Being manager, Mr Stern was allowed to buy clothes at special discount prices.

"And he very kindly let me have his discount for the month, you see, Tim," explained Mum.

"But the handbag and the jewellery were presents," added Mr Stern, "for a very special lady," he said, putting his hand on Mum's hand. Mum didn't go red. She just smiled at him, then at me.

"I'm sorry, Tim, it was my fault really. I should have told you I'd met someone, but ..." she hesitated, "I didn't know how you'd react so I was leaving it a while."

Here Mr Stern interrupted. "But one thing we don't want to leave for a while is you calling me by my first name. You can't go on saying Mr Stern. You must call me Richard."

My mind was doing fast excited somersaults.

"Can I call you Ricky, short for Richard?" I asked him.

Mr Stern looked a bit taken aback but recovered quickly.

"Y-yes, of course. I don't think I've ever been called Ricky before. It'll be quite a novel experience!"

"Great!" I said with a big grin, while Mum eyed me half suspiciously, half happily – if you can imagine that.

Ricky didn't look at all like a boyfriend, but then I suppose Mum didn't look much like someone's girlfriend either.

We played bowls in the pub garden with a plastic set that Ricky got out of his car. While he was getting them Mum whispered to me, "Richard plays bowls for the county, Tim. In fact he's thinking of turning professional soon."

"What, and giving up being Debenhams' manager?"

"That's right."

"So you *could* say he's famous then?"

"Well, only a bit ..."

Well, what an ace Bradford Branch! Ricky Stern is Mum's friend and he's famous. Suddenly everything was Binkydando (perfect).

The bowls was good fun and Ricky was ace at it. No wonder.

Halfway through, Shane walked past the hedge of the pub garden.

"Wotcher, Tim!" he called.

"A friend of yours?" Ricky asked me, and I nodded.

"Come and join us," Ricky called over to Shane.

"This is our friend Ricky Stern," I told Shane. "He's a famous bowler," I whispered.

"What did you say his name was?" Shane whispered back.

"Ricky Stern."

Shane let out a long–drawn–out noise. "Just wait till I tell Jammy, the blanko," he said. "Jammy's spreading it round that you know Ricky *Stone*, the singer."

"Oh, don't be too hard on Jammy," I said generously, "Stern and Stone *do* sound quite similar. Only he must be pretty blatant if he thought I was friends with Ricky *Stone*," I added, which cancelled out my niceness.

After a game of bowls between all four of us we walked home, Shane and I lagging behind.

"Guess what," Shane said, sounding brinked. "We're moving to Farlington. Dad's been appointed chief librarian at Farlington Library."

"Where's that?"

"Miles away. I don't want to go. In fact I think I'll run away on the day they move, then they'll just have to go without me."

I felt sorry for Shane, and I felt sorry for

me. I didn't want him to move. What a bod-ger! It totally ruined my Bradford Branch.

10

Pushty's Revenge

The next day after assembly Pushty grabbed me and said, "Cloakroom, morning break. Okay, Scraggy?"

I nodded and felt sick. This must be my punishment for Lisa's straight talking last week.

If Pushty wanted to see you, you had to see him, so I was in that cloakroom the moment the bell went. After about fifteen minutes, when he'd still not arrived, I wondered whether it would be safe to leave. I decided I'd just give it two more minutes. I started slowly counting the seconds out loud. Pushty walked in on fifty-four.

"Practising counting, Scraggy?"

"Just filling the time," I said.

"Well, here's another time-filler. I hear you're very good at writing songs, and I know someone important who'd like to hear your songs, so write them all down for me tonight and give them to me tomorrow morning break in here. Got it, Scraggy?"

"Okay, Pushty, yeah, okay."

I went outside for the last five minutes of break feeling quite buzzy. Pushty wanted my songs for someone important. I wondered who it could be. I decided to pluck up courage and ask him who it was when I saw him the next day. Jammy and Shane were looking out for me.

"What did he want?" asked Jammy, rushing over to me.

"He only wants me to write down my songs

so he can show them to someone important," I told him.

"Cor! I thought he wanted your head in one of the sinks with the cold tap full on and water running down your shirt," said Jammy in a matter-of-fact voice. "What did you think he wanted, Shane?"

"I think Tim's stupid if he gives anything to Pushty, but especially his own made-up songs," answered Shane.

"Why?" I asked in amazement, because I thought Shane and Jammy would think it was great news.

"Because Pushty's a blegg!" (That's the worst thing you can say about anybody, by the way.) "He'll probably show them to someone important and say that *he* made them up, knowing Pushty."

Although I hated to admit it, I thought Shane was probably right.

"I could copy out all the lyrics from Mum's

old Paul McCartney records and give him those and, you know, say they're mine."

"I somehow think he might just spot the difference between Paul McCartney and Tim Scragg lyrics," said Shane sarcastically. "No, there's only one thing you can do and that's copyright your songs," he finished.

"How?"

"We'll do it in the lunch break."

So during the lunch break I recited all the words of all my songs I could remember while Shane and Jammy copied them out so we had two copies of every song, then Shane wrote TIMOTHY SCRAGG ORIGINAL SONGS 15th JUNE COPYRIGHT on the inside of the envelope and put his own address on the front.

"Now we've just got to pinch a first-class stamp from the office, then bung this in the post so it gets to me by tomorrow morning," went on Shane. "That's how you copyright things. Dad told me. The date on the postmark proves that you made up the songs before Pushty could have done. I'll keep the package sealed, then if ever you have to prove it you can. The other copies of the songs you give to Pushty tomorrow, but only when you definitely know I've received the package safely."

"Burnt out," I said. "Good thinking, Shane." (I wished it was Pushty going to Farlington instead of Shane.)

We tossed a sharpener to see which of us was going to be the one to go and pinch a first-class stamp from the secretary's office. It landed on scratched side up – me. Shane had already said he wasn't going to because he'd done enough, actually thinking up the plan, and Jammy was the lucky brain who'd chosen smooth side up.

The secretary always went to lunch at half-past one, after everybody else, so I knew her office would be empty. But just in case, I decided to nudge the door open very slowly with my foot. I was right in the middle of the slow-motion door-opening technique when it was suddenly yanked open from the inside, and there stood Miss Rigid Bottom. It was only my foot pressing on the door that had kept my balance, so when the door wasn't there any more I fell over.

I scrambled to my feet and Rigid Bottom bent down with a bit of creaking and picked up the envelope with all my songs in it that I'd dropped.

"What on earth are you doing, Tim? And what do you want?" she asked without handing back my envelope. I had to think quickly.

"I wanted to show you my songs," I said. "You see, I saw you come in here, so ..." I trailed off.

"Well, well! I had no idea you made up your own material, Tim. I'd love to see them. Why has this got Shane's name on it, though?"

"Because they're quite precious so I'm copyrighting them. Shane's never going to unseal the envelope and the postmark proves when I wrote them."

"Good idea," said Miss Ridge with a beam. "Tell you what, I'll read through them then I'll stick a stamp on and pop them in the post this afternoon. Okay?"

"Yes, thank you very much, Miss Ridge, and could you make it a first-class stamp, please?"

"Certainly."

It was true what the vicar said – God *does* move in mysterious ways.

In morning break the next day I handed over the second copies of the songs to Pushty. Shane had nodded at me in assembly, which was how we'd agreed he would let me know he'd received the package.

"Thank you, Scraggy," said Pushty, flicking through the pages of lyrics with a sniggery smile on his face. "And I've no doubt you'll be hearing from the very important person I mentioned in no time at all."

"You will tell them I wrote the songs, won't you, Pushty?" I asked fearfully.

"I certainly will. I shall take absolutely no credit for a single word, Scraggy. Never you fear."

He walked away laughing, and I tried to ignore the uncomfortable feeling I had.

Just two days later in morning break, the very important person called me to see her in her office. Her face was stern, her lips were set. My songs were on her desk.

"Timothy Scragg," said Mrs Williams, the headmistress, in a very tight voice, "I have *never* read such a load of garbage as this!" She picked up my songs and slapped them down hard on her desk.

"How *dare* you apply such insults to your teachers? I am ashamed that anyone from this school should commit such disgusting words to paper and call them songs, and I can assure you, you will regret the day you ever composed this trash, when I've finished with you."

I just stared at her. I couldn't understand what was wrong with the songs. I knew I'd got "puke" and "spew" in the first song, but I didn't think they were very bad words and I certainly hadn't said anything insulting about the teachers.

"Here," she said, thrusting the top paper under my nose. "Sing this one out loud and see how it makes you feel. I believe it is to the tune of The Grand Old Duke of York. Go on, off you go."

I looked at the paper. This wasn't my handwriting. It was similar to my handwriting, but it wasn't exactly the same. I looked at the page. It was awful. I didn't know what to do. Pushty had changed all the words, made them really rude. But Pushty would kill me if I said it was him, and anyway Mrs Williams would never believe me because the handwriting match was so good.

"Timothy!"

There was nothing for it. I just had to sing.

> "Oh, Miss Rigid Bottom Ridge,
> She bummed about all day,
> She sang some randy songs and then
> Her corset came away ..."

I stopped and tried to speak but my voice was getting stuck in my throat.

"I didn't make this up, honestly Mrs Williams. My song's all about the Blatant Duke of York ..."

"Is this your handwriting, Tim?"

"Someone's tried to imitate it —"

"Don't try to blame someone else. I can see by comparing this English book of yours with this trash, that it *is* your handwriting."

"Yes, but —"

"You will stay in every break till the end of

146

term. You will have detention every Monday until the end of term and you will *not* be in the end-of-term play. You may go back to the classroom now for the rest of break."

I went straight to the cloakroom like a zombie. My hands were sweating. I rinsed them under the cold tap for ages, then left the cloakroom without bothering to dry them.

Pushty was blocking my way.

"Hello, Scraggy," he said with a leer. "There's something I've been meaning to tell you."

He took a letter out of his pocket and read it out to me in a stupid kid's voice, and the more he read, the more I felt like crying. I forced the tears back by swallowing and swallowing as he read out an exact copy of the letter I had received from *Jim'll Fix It*. When he'd finished he laughed, and Foggs and Steve, who were standing just behind him, laughed too.

"Familiar, Scraggs?"

He didn't wait for an answer. I stared at him, still swallowing like mad.

"So now you know. It was good old Pushty who wrote to you from *Jim'll Fix It*. In fact I fixed it for you good and proper, didn't I? And you thought you were going to be famous!"

Pushty suddenly grabbed my collar and yanked me off my feet. My nose was about two centimetres away from his.

"Now don't you *ever* accuse me of shop-lifting again, and don't let me see you talking to that lippy little Lisa again either. I don't like her sharp tongue. Got it, Scraggy?"

He put me down and turned to Foggs and Steve.

"Come on, let's leave him alone to have a little weep."

And out they all went. Foggs turned round at the door and gave me a strange worried look before he scuttled off after his hateful hero. I went into the toilet and flushed it so no one would hear me crying.

After a couple of minutes I washed my face and walked slowly down the corridor towards the science lab. It was science next lesson and I thought I'd just wait in the lab for Mrs Jones.

I'd hardly set off when I heard Lisa's voice coming from her classroom. She was really yelling at someone. The door to the classroom was open. I stood in the doorway. Lisa was shouting at the top of her voice at Pushty. She was shaking with anger. Neither of them saw me.

"You've got to be a real blurg to do something like that, Pushty. But then that's what you are, aren't you? A blurg of the first order."

Lisa stood there, eyes blazing, body shaking, then a second later she was staggering back clutching at a chair before she hit her head on a desk and fell to the ground. She lay there, white and still. Pushty was looking at his fist as though it had nothing to do with him and hadn't asked his permission before lashing out at Lisa. I'd never hated anyone as much as I hated Pushty at that moment.

I belted to the staff room to get help and nearly collided with Mrs Williams.

"Mrs Williams, come quick! Pushty's bashed Lisa's face and knocked her out!" I grabbed Mrs Williams' sleeve and pulled her along.

She looked very worried, and when she saw Lisa she went totally white and knelt down beside her.

"Oh, my God!" she whispered. "Tim, go to the staff room as fast as possible and get Mrs Nicholas and Mrs Jones."

I ran all the way and came back with both teachers. Mrs Jones knelt down and felt Lisa's wrist and neck then her head. She took off her own cardigan and gently put it under Lisa's head. Mrs Williams was whispering to Mrs

Nicholas about phoning Lisa's parents and an ambulance.

"Now tell me exactly what happened, Tim," said Mrs Williams. She sat on a chair and pulled out another one for me and looked at me very intently.

"Is Lisa going to be okay?" I asked in a whisper.

"Yes, she'll be well looked after at hospital, don't worry. Can you tell me what happened, Tim?"

"Well, I was just walking to the science lab to wait for Mrs Jones when I heard Lisa's voice really shouting. It was coming from in here so I looked in and there was Lisa yelling at Pushty; she was calling him ... you know, names, and Pushty punched her face. She staggered backwards a bit then she fell over and hit her head on the desk. It all happened very quickly, especially when he hit her."

Mrs Williams looked around.

"So where is Pushty now? He didn't come

out of this door, and I've been here ever since – so where is he?"

I looked round wildly, hoping I'd see Pushty flattened against a cupboard or hanging from the light. There was a window open and we were on the ground floor. It was obvious how he'd got away but I didn't think Mrs Williams would believe me. She'd really got it in for me.

"She's stirring a bit," said Mrs Jones softly and we all leaned forwards. I expected Lisa to mumble "Where am I?" or "What happened?" but she didn't, she just sat up as though she'd woken from a good night's sleep and then remembered a bad dream.

"Where's Pushty?" she asked me.

"I'm not sure," I answered carefully.

Then Lisa must have realized she was lying on the classroom floor with Mrs Williams and Mrs Jones bending over her. Her eyes looked panicky.

"Just keep still, dear," said Mrs Jones.

"You've had a bad fall and you're going to hospital just to check there's no damage."

Mrs Williams held Lisa's hand and smiled at her.

"Can you remember what happened, Lisa?"

"Pushty punched me in the face because I called him a – a –"

"Well, never mind what you called him. Why did you call him it?"

"Because I was in here sorting out the posters for Mrs Nicholas, when I heard him talking outside that window. He was boasting to someone about this letter he'd written to Tim ..." Lisa interrupted herself to say, "Sorry, Tim, but you'll have to know some-time."

"It's okay," I said. "Pushty's told me himself."

"Told you what?" Mrs Williams asked me.

"Well you see, Tim wrote to *Jim'll Fix It* ages ago," Lisa carried on for me, "and

Pushty got to hear about it, and for a joke he replied to Tim's letter pretending it was from *Jim'll Fix It* and saying Tim's Fix-It idea had been accepted and Tim was going to be on TV, but it was all a trick. Tim's been excited about it for weeks. He was going to sing his songs in a concert, but now it's not going to happen. That's why I was so angry with Pushty. And he climbed in through the window, but I wasn't scared. I told him what a low-down, hateful thing he'd done, and that's when he must have hit me."

Lisa jerked her head up.

"Take it gently," said Mrs Jones. "The ambulance'll be here in a minute."

But Lisa jumped up and sat on the desk with me.

"I'm okay now, honestly," she said, touching her head. Her eyes suddenly went wide.

"Wow! What's that?"

She picked up my hand and rubbed it on her head. I'd never felt such a huge bump.

"Borgonzola! It's like a melon!"

Mrs Williams and Mrs Jones laughed and Miss Ridge came in.

"The ambulance is here —"

She stopped and looked in surprise at Lisa. "Sitting up already? That's good. Mrs Nicholas is just talking to your mum on the phone. Your mum's going straight to the hospital. She'll meet you there."

"I'll just tell her you're up and about," said Mrs Jones, rushing out of the classroom, "in case she's worrying."

"Oh, no, not an ambulance," said Lisa, looking embarrassed.

"Well, you didn't think we were going to let you *walk* to hospital, did you?" asked Miss Ridge.

"I wish I could. Can Tim come too? We could sing one of your songs, Tim."

Lisa laughed and started marching round the room.

"Oh, the blatant Duke of York ..." she

sang and Miss Ridge joined in clapping and singing, "He buzzed about all day; he sang some bandy songs and then a bodger came his way ..."

"Come on!" laughed Miss Ridge. "Mrs Williams is going to think we're all mad – and anyway, the ambulance is waiting."

Miss Ridge went out with her arm round Lisa and I was left alone with Mrs Williams. She spoke to me very softly.

"I think I owe you an apology. I hadn't realized Miss Ridge was acquainted with the Blatant Duke of York."

She stopped talking and looked very serious.

"Have you any idea who it was who changed the words of that song, Tim, and imitated your handwriting so effectively?"

I only hesitated for a second.

"It was Pushty. He said he was going to show the songs to someone important. I thought he meant a famous person who might want to record them. That's why I gave them to Pushty, only don't tell him ..."

"I shall be dealing severely with that boy, Tim. You won't have to worry about him again. Now if you run, you'll catch up with Lisa. I should think she'd like your company in the ambulance."

"Cor! Thanks, Mrs Williams!"

Pushty was expelled. As well as hitting Lisa and trying to get me into trouble with the songs, he'd been blackmailing Foggs for ages and had stolen money from at least two teachers. Lisa's head was okay apart from the enormous bump that took over a week to go down.

A couple of days later Shane, Jammy and I were walking home from school when Lisa caught up with us.

"What was that word you called Pushty, Lisa?" I asked her.

"A blurg," she told us.

"That's a brilliant B Club word, don't you think, Shane?" said Jammy.

"Yeah," said Shane, trying not to show too much enthusiasm.

"Tim and me were wondering about Lisa joining the B Club," Jammy went on.

"We'd have to take a vote on it," said Shane.

Jammy and I stuck our hands up in the air and said "*In*!"

Shane would have looked pretty stupid if he'd not agreed.

"*In*!" he said.

Lisa winked at me.

I winked back.

Shane didn't notice.

Jammy did. He tried to do two winks at the same time, but it came out as a blink.

Good old Jammy!

11

Interviews

I can't believe it's four months since the last time I listened in on one of Mum and Pat's conversations. Yesterday I heard them talking again. I immediately called a meeting of the B Club and told them what I'd heard.

"What do you mean?" Shane asked. "Ricky's got another girlfriend as well as your mum?"

"Well, that's what it sounded like," I answered. "Someone called Jessie."

"Don't jump to conclusions," said Lisa,

frowning. "Jessie could be Ricky's mother or his cleaner or something."

"Well," said Shane, "sounds to me like something that needs investigating."

I looked at Lisa a bit uncertainly.

"Don't let's go rushing into anything," she advised.

"We could try the pebble-kicking test to see what Jessie's like," suggested Jammy.

"Huh! Boring," said Shane.

"Well, it's not very accurate but it *is* good fun. Come on, let's try it."

So we all trooped outside and Jammy said, "Let's see how old she is by how far the pebble goes."

"Here's a stone," said Lisa, plonking a huge sharp-looking object by my right big toe.

"That rhododendron bush means really old," said Shane, beginning to get into it, "and those spiky pink flowers mean grown up but younger than your mum, and if it doesn't even get that far, she's young like us."

"Go on, Tim," yelled Jammy. "Kick!"

And I did. "YOWWWCH!"

The stone was far too big to kick and my trainer was far too thin to stop my big toe getting cut.

"Borgonzola!" I yelled, sitting down on the back doorstep and pulling my trainer off. My sock was all bloody.

"I'll get you a plaster," said Lisa, and she found one in the bathroom cupboard and stuck it on my toe in no time at all.

We looked out of the kitchen window. The stone had gone less than a metre.

"Jessie's not very old then," said Lisa with a smile.

"About two, judging from that performance," laughed Shane.

"Right, that's that sorted out. What other matters have we got to discuss this week?" asked Lisa, who liked the meetings to be done properly.

"One more thing," I said, and I explained

that Bear was going back to France soon, and that when I'd asked Mum if we were getting another lodger, she'd said, "Well, I don't know; Bear's such a tough act to follow." It was obvious Mum thought no one could be such a nice lodger as Bear, but I thought if we advertised, we could interview everyone ourselves and choose the best one, then give Mum a nice surprise when we'd chosen one.

Shane said, "Good idea, Tim. We'll carry out the short–listing and selection process."

Shane knows all about short–listing and selection because it's what his dad has just been through. Shane's dad has been short-listed and selected to run the Farlington Library. That's why Shane's got to move to Farlington. He loves books, does Shane's dad, and he's a good jokey sort of father because he's always comparing real life to books. You see, if real life comes off more boring than books, then he changes real life to make it more exciting – that's what Douglas Plant told Shane anyway.

So this is the advert that me, Jammy, Shane and Lisa made up after a lot of hard work in Jammy's shed:

WANTED
PERSON TO LODGE WITH SMALL FAMILY
FROM BEGINNING OF AUGUST.
PLEASE APPLY BOX NUMBER 100

We decided a box number was better than putting our phone number because we didn't want Mum answering the phone and spoiling the surprise. So the advert went in the paper and we all waited, feeling nervous and excited at the same time.

Three people answered the advert. Jammy, Shane and I were due to interview the first of these possible lodgers at ten o'clock on Saturday morning, the next at a quarter past ten and the third at half-past. Lisa couldn't do the interviewing because she had to go out with her mum.

Mum was supposed to be going out to work, but at half-past nine I got the shock of my life when she suddenly announced that she wasn't going because the bookshop was changing hands and being redecorated. Mum looked quite sad and said she didn't think she would be able to keep her part-time job. I said to Jammy, "What are we going to do? Mum's not going to the bookshop after all."

"We'll just have to invent some reason why she's got to go out," said Jammy. "I know," he went on, "I'll phone her up, pretending to be my mum, and invite her round for coffee at my house."

"Just one little problem," said Shane.

"What?" asked Jammy.

"When Tim's mum turns up at your place, your mum's going to wonder what on earth she's doing there."

"Yeah, that's no good," I agreed. "Mum

would be really suspicious; she'd come straight back home."

"I've got a great bangler," said Shane. "Has your mum got any library books?"

"Yes," I answered, "she's got loads."

"Right, go and get one that you think she's read," ordered Shane.

I belted upstairs and came down with something called *Rebuilding Coventry* by Sue Townsend. I knew Mum had read that because I'd heard her raving about it to Pat on the phone.

"Right, Jammy, your house is nearest," instructed Shane. "Go home and phone Tim's mum, pretending you're from the library. Say something like 'Good morning, could I speak to Mrs Scragg, please?' and then Tim's mum will say, 'Yes, this is Mrs Scragg,' and you say 'Ah, Mrs Scragg, have you by any chance got the book entitled *Rebuilding Coventry* by Sue Townsend?' and then Tim's mum will say 'Yes, I have,' and you say 'Ah, well, Mrs Scragg, I wonder if we could possibly have it back as soon as possible because another customer has specially requested it.'"

Shane grinned at us both as if to say, "Great idea, isn't it?" but Jammy's mouth was looking droopy.

"Borgonzola, Shane," he said, "I'll never remember that lot."

"Why don't *you* make the phone call from Jammy's house, Shane?" I suggested. "Only you'd better be quick about it; we've got to get Mum out of the house before the first lodger turns up."

"Right, come on Jammy, let's get going," said Shane. "Oh, and Tim, when your mum says she's going to the library, you say, 'Oh, good. Could you get me a book about boss-eyed badgers for school?'"

Jammy was looking a bit puzzled.

"Boss-eyed badgers? There's no such thing, is there?"

"Course there isn't," answered Shane, "so

it's going to take Tim's mum an awfully long time to find one, isn't it? So she's going to be out of the house for ages, isn't she?"

"Bangler!" I answered.

"Right, see you soon, Tim," Shane said, grabbing Jammy's arm and pulling him out of the back door.

It was a really funny feeling sitting at home waiting for the phone to ring. It rang almost straight away and I leapt into the sitting room as Mum answered it. I could tell it wasn't Shane because Mum said she'd love a cutting. It was probably Pat. Mum and Pat were forever swopping plant cuttings. After about ten minutes, when she was still on the phone, I began to get worried about the time, so I wrote a little note and thrust it under her nose. It said, "Could you get off the phone, please?"

Mum didn't look too pleased when she read it, but she got off the phone amazingly quickly and said, "That's a bit rude, Tim."

"Sorry, Mum. I'm expecting Jammy to

phone about this project we're doing – on boss-eyed badgers."

At that moment the phone rang. I held my breath and looked at it.

"Well, go on then," said Mum, "answer it. That'll be Jammy, I expect."

Borgonzola! I really wanted Mum to answer it.

"Hello," I said, "Tim here."

Mum looked at me as though I was bonkers when I said that, because I don't know about you, but I normally just say "Hello" when I answer the phone.

Shane's voice came over loud and clear. "What are *you* doing answering it, you blanko? Where's your mum?"

"Yes, just a minute, I'll get her," I said in a very deliberate voice. Shane giggled so I handed Mum the phone really slowly to give him time to stop.

"Yes …" Mum was saying to Shane, sounding a bit uncertain. "No-o …" she said, sounding very uncertain. I wished I could hear Shane's lady's voice at the other end. "Oh, you mean Rebuilding *Coventry*, not *Birmingham* ... Yes, I've got that ..."

She was smiling into the mouthpiece so I thought Shane must be doing all right even if he *did* blimp the title.

"No, that's all right," Mum was saying, "I've finished it." Then she sounded a bit surprised. "You want it *today*? Well, I could ... Look, I'll tell you what, I'll pop down with it straight away." (Pause) "No problem at all ... See you soon, bye."

Burnt out! Good old Shane.

"That was the library," Mum said to me. "Another customer desperately wants my book for a course she's doing or something. I must say it's most unusual for the library to phone people up and actually ask to have a book back when it's not even overdue. I suppose it must be a particularly popular book."

Mum went upstairs and came down again about twenty seconds later.

"That's funny, it isn't there," she said. "I definitely left it by my bed. Have you seen it, Tim?"

A bodger came creeping round my brain. Course I'd seen it. It was in the kitchen where we'd left it, wasn't it? I had to think quickly.

"Oh yes, I saw it by your bed, and we're doing all about Coventry at school, so I had a look at it."

"And did you learn much about Coventry, Tim?" Mum asked in a voice that sounded like she was about to catch me out.

I hesitated then carefully said, "Um, no, not really. The book wasn't really about that, was it?"

"The book was about a *woman* called Coventry."

"Yes, I thought it was. And Mum, you know the other project we're doing at school at the moment – about the boss-eyed badgers?

170

Well, I was wondering if you could see if they've got any books about them in the library while you're there."

"Boss-eyed badgers! Oh, come on, Tim, you've definitely got that wrong. Is it supposed to be bog-eyed badgers or black-eyed badgers or something?"

"No, it was definitely boss-eyed badgers."

"Well, I'll have a quick look, but I can tell you now I'm not spending my time doing your homework, Tim."

So Mum eventually went out at five to ten and Shane and Jammy were back as soon as she'd gone. We all sat along one side of the kitchen table with pen and paper in front of us (which gives you an important feeling, I can tell you). There was also a jug of water and four glasses in the middle of the table. Shane said he'd often seen jugs of water and glasses on the table when people had interviews on TV chat shows.

We'd written down two questions each to

ask the lodgers. My questions were: 1) Do you bathe often? and 2) Do you eat breakfast early or late? Jammy's questions were: 1) Are you fussy about food? and 2) Do you go out much? Shane's questions sounded more businesslike: 1) What's your job? and 2) Are you good at paying rent on time?

I also thought one of us had better ask "Have you got loads of friends who might keep coming round all the time?" (Because after all, Mum and I didn't want the house full of people in case we were doing something private like miming to Ricky Stone records.)

At ten o'clock on the dot the front doorbell rang. Shane said, "Quick, Jammy, write down 'very punctual' while Tim lets him in." I went to answer the door, feeling quite nervous. It was a tall lady with bright orange curly hair, enormous sunglasses, a big spotty scarf tied round her chin and loads of jangly bracelets right up her arms. She looked about twenty-five but it was difficult to tell because of the glasses. Her lips were so shiny I could practically see my reflection in them.

"Come in," I said, trying to sound in charge. She didn't look at all surprised to see a boy there. She followed me into the kitchen and sat down opposite me, Shane and Jammy. I looked at Jammy. His mouth was hanging open in surprise at Shiny Lips. Shane's eyes looked as though he was about to bore a hole through the lady. She herself was looking around.

"Where's your mother, boy?" she said to me. "If I'm to lodge here I shall need to meet your mother, shall I not?"

"His mother doesn't wish to be involved until the short-listing has been completed, and we are here for that very purpose actually," said Shane in a really posh voice. It sounded dead clever what Shane said. I was glad to have him there, I can tell you. Jammy's mouth was still hanging open, only now he was staring at Shane.

"Am I to take it there are other candidates for the role?" asked Shiny Lips. She still hadn't taken her dark glasses off.

Just as she said that there was a knock at the back door. I opened it and there on the doorstep stood a very fat, *very* tall man with a mutton-chop moustache, extremely bushy eyebrows and a great grey beard. He spoke with a Scottish accent.

"Have I got the right place where you're wantin' a lodger now, lad?"

"Well, yes," I answered, and turned round to Shane for help. After all, we didn't want to interview two at once.

"That's okay," said Shane very confidently, "we'll see these two together." The man had come in and was puffing and panting along to our kitchen table. I was just about to shut the back door when a strong American-accented voice came floating in from outside.

"Hey, hold on there, kid! Bethanne Ewing from the US of A at your service. And liddle ole Bethy is here to see about this liddle ole advert. What a quaint liddle place you have here."

She pushed the door open wide and strolled into the kitchen. She was wearing a titchy miniskirt and a pair of white boots past her knees. Her top half looked like she'd forgotten her jumper. She'd got one of those pointy bra things. I'd never seen anyone wearing one of those before except on telly. The other thing she had on was an enormous sunhat that covered half her face.

"Come in," I said, looking desperately at Shane. Shane didn't look or sound quite so confident by this stage. He told me to get another chair from the other room, which I did, and we all sat down. Jammy's mouth was still hanging open. He was staring at Bethanne's chest. It was really embarrassing.

"Go on, you start," said Shane, elbowing me in the side.

"Right," I said, looking at my paper. I

turned to Shiny Lips and said, "Do you bathe often?"

She looked at me as though I was a bit of dirt and said, "You watch your tongue, young man!"

Bethanne and Mutton Chops both tittered.

"He's only asking because there's only one bathroom," said Jammy, quite helpfully for him, but even with Jammy's help I was feeling like blimping the whole thing because I knew straight away that none of these people would be any good as a lodger. The problem was having to tell them. I'd just have to carry on with the questions, then tell them all that I'd let them know later by phoning them or something.

"*You* ask something," I hissed at Shane.

"What's your job?" Shane asked Bethanne.

"I'm a model, sunshine," she answered with a big smile and a toss of her hair. "And I sometimes model in the bathroom," she said, turning to me, "but don't worry, sweetheart, I won't model in *your* bathroom." And she did a big pouty look as though I'd got a camera or something. I tried to stop myself going red but it was no good.

"I like a bath myself," said Mutton Chops with the Scottish accent. "A good old bath, night and morning, stays the sweat and stops the yawning," he added, which really amused the two ladies. Shiny Lips nearly fell off her chair she was laughing so much.

Shane was writing furiously on his paper. I was quite impressed with Shane, I must say, until I looked over his shoulder, and saw he'd just written loads of wiggly lines.

"*You* ask something," Shane told Jammy, and Jammy asked Shiny Lips if she was fussy about food.

"Oh no," Shiny Lips answered. "I'll eat anything. Food is my passion. Generally I eat bacon, eggs, sausage, chips and beans for breakfast, but I could just as well eat plenty of whatever you've got."

I don't know if it was the mention of all that food, but I suddenly began to feel a bit sick. "I'm on a crash diet," said Bethanne. "I just have half a grapefruit for breakfast, and some black coffee."

"I like a bowl of Scotch Porridge Oats myself," said Mutton Chops. "And in the evening I cut out the porridge and just have the Scotch."

When he said that, all three of them fell about laughing again. It reminded me of something but I didn't have the time to think what, because the back door opened and there stood Mum and Ricky!

12

Bradford Branches

Mum and Ricky stared at Bethanne, Shiny Lips and Mutton Chops for about five seconds while there was dead silence in the room. Then Mum spoke.

"What's going on, Tim?" she asked with a nervous twitchy smile.

I thought Bethanne or one of the others might answer but none of them breathed a word.

"It was ... supposed to be a ... surprise, Mum. I was trying ... to get you a new lodger, you see ... as Bear's going soon ..."

I faded out because I didn't know what else to say. Mum looked at Ricky as if to say, "What shall we do?"

As calmly as anything Ricky said to the three visitors, "Actually, Mrs Scragg has filled the vacancy, thank you. I am her new lodger, so we're sorry to disappoint you all. The news obviously hadn't filtered through to Tim here, but ..." Ricky shrugged his shoulders and gave them all a big smile "... but there it is. Thank you all the same for troubling to come, and I hope you're sucessful elsewhere."

Ricky held open the kitchen door in a broad hint for Bethanne and the others to go, but they just sat there and looked at each other, grinning. Then Mutton Chops suddenly peeled his moustache and beard off, and at the same time Bethanne took off her hat, and Shiny Lips took her dark glasses and wig off, and there before us sat Douglas, Sheena and Claire Plant!

"But—" I said.

"So it was *you* all the time!" Jammy said, before his mouth fell open again.

"You rotten bleggs!" said Shane, jumping up from his chair and looking absolutely furious. "How did you know the advert came from us anyway?" he asked.

"We're sorry, Shane," laughed Sheena, pulling a tissue out of her handbag and wiping her shiny lipstick off. "We just couldn't resist dressing up and coming along to fool you. You see, we were tipped off by a friend of yours."

And in walked Lisa!

"I thought you had to go out with your mum—" I began accusingly.

"Rotten trick," said Shane, scowling.

"What d'yer do that for, Lisa? I thought you were one of us," added Jammy, looking a bit upset.

"I'm sorry," said Lisa, through giggles, "I had to do *something*. I mean it's obvious your mum doesn't want a lodger now she's got Ricky, isn't it?"

"You must admit it was a good disguise," grinned Douglas.

"And brilliant acting," added Claire in her American accent, grabbing Sheena's spotty scarf and putting it round her shoulders to cover her chest up.

Ricky was looking at Mum for an explanation. His hand had dropped down from the open back door and his face wore a puzzled expression. Mum hadn't moved a muscle. As we watched, her mouth began to twitch, then without any other warning she let out a great bellow of a laugh and fell on to Ricky, who had to hold her up she was laughing so much.

"It's another of Tim's brainwaves gone wrong," spluttered Mum. "And how!" she laughed, pointing at the Plants. "Thank goodness you're not really prospective lodgers," she carried on between laughs, and suddenly everyone was laughing. Poor Ricky must have thought he'd entered a madhouse. Mum began to introduce him.

"Ricky, you've already met Tim's friend Shane, well, now meet Shane's sisters, Claire and Sheena, and his brother, Douglas – the Plant family en masse."

"How do you do?" said Ricky, grinning at them all, now he understood the joke.

"And I'm Jammy," said Jammy.

"Pleased to meet you, Jammy," said Ricky.

"And this is Lisa," I finished off.

Lisa and Ricky smiled at each other, then Ricky introduced himself.

"Well, everybody, I'm *not* the new lodger. I was just trying to help Tim out of a tight spot."

"That was a real Bradford Branch, wasn't it, Tim?" said Jammy.

"But not for you lot," said Shane to his family. "You're *for* it!"

"Let's have some coffee," Mum suggested, then she suddenly swung round to me.

"Incidentally, Tim, the lady at the library knew nothing about the phonecall I received from there this morning, which is odd, wouldn't you say, because she'd been there all morning."

Shane and I exchanged glances.

"Sorry, Mrs Scragg," said Shane. "It was me really. You see we had to get you out of the house and that was all we could think of."

"Well, what a ratbag!" said Claire Plant, ruffling her brother's hair. "I don't know where you get these crazy ideas from!"

Everybody laughed including Mum. Mum looked really happy. I didn't think I'd ever seen her looking so happy. She put the kettle on, then when everybody was sitting down and talking, she nodded at me as if to say, "Come in the other room, I've got something to tell you."

I followed her out and we sat in the hall on the bottom stair.

"Tim, Ricky wants to marry me ..." She paused and looked at me carefully.

"Yea, bangler!" I said.

"Hang on, love, I want to be sure you're in agreement before I say yes."

"Course I'm in agreement."

"We'd live in his house in Brinton Road, but nothing else would change at all except you'd have a man around who you *might* want to call Dad one day—"

"And who *might* be the Number One bowls player for England one day?"

"Well, yes," said Mum, "but that's not really the point ... and Tim, there's one other thing ..."

But I didn't care. I ran into the kitchen and said to Jammy, Shane and Lisa, "Guess what? Mum's marrying Ricky!"

Mum was right behind me.

"Tim," she said, sounding a bit embarrassed, but Ricky put his arm round her and the other arm round me and said, "Well, it saved us making a formal announcement, Marg," and everybody laughed and said "Congratulations" loads of times.

"Oh, just a minute," said Ricky.

He went out and came back a moment later holding a little girl of about two in his arms. She was rubbing her eyes and yawning like mad.

"This is Jessie, my daughter. She was fast asleep when we arrived just now, so I let her sleep on in the car."

"Jessie!" screeched the whole B Club in astonishment. We were all picturing that sharp stone that had moved about ten centimetres when I kicked it. It was Lisa who asked the six-million-dollar question.

"How old is she?"

"Jessie?" said Rick. "She's . . . let me see . . . she's two."

Well, that did it! Shane did a huge war whoop and we all slapped each other's hands and said things like "Burnt out!" and

"Bangler" and "Well done, Signor Psychic Scraggini!"

Ricky shook his head in bewilderment, and Mum spluttered, "Sorry about this, Richard; I've never understood their language or how their minds work. But while everybody's in such a festive mood, why don't we have lunch here to celebrate?"

So Mum got on the phone and invited Pat and all Lisa's family, Jammy's family and Shane's parents. They all turned up along with Bear, and everybody brought some food with them. The only people who said they couldn't come were Shane's parents. Shane looked a bit brinked.

Lunch was great. I don't mean the food, I mean everything. The adults started jiving in pairs. Lisa's mum and dad were excellent at it. Ricky and Mum kept falling over, Jammy's mum and dad hadn't got a clue and as for Pat and Bear, I've never seen anything so hilarious in my life.

Then Bear made a sort of funny thank-you speech to Mum for having him as a lodger. Everybody clapped like mad at the end of it.

Then Jammy's dad organized the Hokey Cokey. Normally I hate things like that, but it was so funny watching Dora and Jessie, their fat legs waddling, their nappies nearly falling down; and you should have heard Bear ... "Ah, Ahki Khaki Khako!" There was only one more week before Janine was expecting him halfway up the aisle in some French church or other. I thought I was probably going to miss him with his strong accent and his even stronger aftershave.

At the end of the Hokey Cokey, the door was flung open and who should walk in but Shane's mum and dad.

"Guess what?" said Mr Plant.

"What?" asked Shane suspiciously.

"Farlington's off!"

"I wondered what the smell was," said

Jammy, and Lisa and I clapped because he'd made a good joke without any rehearsals.

"What do you mean, off?" asked Shane cautiously.

"We're not moving away," Mrs Plant explained. "Dad's going to manage the bookshop here in the High Street. It's all settled."

Shane's face went into a huge beam as that big bangler whizzed round and round.

"Burnt out!" I screeched, and jumped on Shane's back. We careered round the kitchen for about two minutes while everybody whooped and clapped.

"I shall be looking for part-time help ..." added Mr Plant with a wink at Mum.

The B Club renamed all the food. Personally, I ate bossages, biche, brisps, beanuts and a big slab of bocolate bake.

"What a messy lot you are over there," said Mum, interrupting our B's. "Look at all those crumbs!"

"You mean bumbs," whispered Shane after she'd gone.

Jammy and I nearly choked laughing. I think I would have if Shane hadn't given me a huge prod in the ribs.

"Look over there!" he hissed.

Ricky and Mum were holding hands and looking gooey.

"Yuk!" I said, although I didn't really mean it.

Lisa saved me as usual.

"Your mum looks really happy, and she deserves it, doesn't she?"

Mum walked over, grinning as though she'd heard us, and dropped two letters in my lap.

"These came today," she said.

"For me!" I ripped the first one open. Mum peered over my shoulder. We read the letter silently. At the end Mum clapped her hands and everybody went quiet.

"Listen to this, everyone." And she read out my letter.

" *'Dear Bill'* (my son's stage name," she explained),

" *'Congratulations! You have been selected to appear on* Jim'll Fix It *on BBC Television.*

" *'One of the team's researchers will phone you within the next fortnight to explain the procedure for filming and to discuss a schedule with you. We understand from your letter that you write your own songs, and would like this to be a special feature of your Fix It.*
With very best wishes,
Yours sincerely,
Amanda Ryan'."

Mum put the letter down and smiled at me. I didn't dare believe it. What if it was another trick of Pushty's?

I must have looked really anxious because everyone was staring at me. They were probably wondering why I wasn't dead pleased about it. But then they didn't know about Pushty, did they? Lisa stood up.

"A little while ago," she began, "Tim got a letter which seemed on the face of it to be from *Jim'll Fix It*. It actually turned out to be a cruel joke. I think we all should have realized at the time because the letter said Dear Tim, and Tim had actually signed himself Bill Brent on his letter to Jimmy Saville. Anyway, this one can't be a hoax because it's addressed to Bill Brent!"

"Three cheers for Tim!" yelled Shane. "I'd better write and tell them to send any other letters to me because I'm going to be your agent, Tim."

The Plant family fell about laughing at that, but as usual Shane didn't notice.

Jammy said, "What about this other letter, Tim?" and I told him I didn't mind if he opened it.

Shane and Lisa started giving Jessie and

Dora races, and quite a few of the grown-ups started making bets on who would win. It was quite funny because Jessie and Dora didn't realize what they had to do at all. Jammy suddenly handed me something. I couldn't believe my eyes. It was a cheque for twenty pounds. There was one for Jammy too, and a little note:

The residents of Leybourne Road want to thank you and your friend for all your hard work during the dustmen's strike. Please find enclosed a token of our appreciation. Hope it's BIN a nice surprise!
Best wishes from us all,
Mrs Hipple (Number 37)

Another Bradford Branch, I thought as Jammy and I examined our cheques. "Keep or share?" I asked him. We looked over at Lisa and Shane then back to each other. "Share," we said at the same moment.

"Good decision," said Mum. I hadn't realized she was right behind me. "Just one more thing," she said with a smile, and she showed me a cheque for a hundred pounds. "I know it says my name on it, but it should really go to you. After all, it was your invention that won first prize."

I must have been looking gormless. I didn't know what she was on about.

"Don't you remember the competition for the household gadget? Well, your laundry ball was the winner. The judges reckoned it could double as a washing basket. So it looks as though you *are* going to have some nice things to wear for your television appearance, doesn't it?"

"Borgonzola!" I said slowly and Mum gave me a smacking great kiss.

I saw Jammy nudge Shane just as Shane was taking a photo of me and Mum. It was going to be one weird lopsided photo when it was developed, but who cares?

"I propose a toast to Tim," said Ricky, raising his glass.

"To Tim," said everybody, raising their glasses.

"Bim!" piped up Jessie.

Well, you know what I'm thinking, don't you?

That's right – definite B Club material!

Glossary of B Words

Bandy – great

Bangler – a sudden good idea

Binkydando – perfect

Blanko – someone who does something really
    stupid

Blatant – stupid and embarrassing

Blegg – the worst thing you can call anyone!

Blimp – to forget whatever it is you're doing,
    because it's useless

Blimpworthy – useless

Blurg – Lisa's version of Blegg

Bodger – a bad thought

Borgonzola – what you say when you're in shock

Bradford Branch – a lucky escape/happy ending

Brinked – totally sad/upset

Bruesome – angry enough for a fight

Burnt Out! – really impressive!

Buzzy – excited and busy at the same time

The Babysitters Club

Need a babysitter? Then call the Babysitters Club. Kristy Thomas and her friends are all experienced sitters. They can tackle any job from rampaging toddlers to a pandemonium of pets. To find out all about them, read on!

Our favourite Babysitters are detectives too! Don't miss the new series of Babysitters Club Mysteries:

Available now:

No 1: Stacey and the Missing Ring
When Stacey's accused of stealing a valuable ring from a new family she's been sitting for, she's devastated – Stacey is *not* a thief!

No 2: Beware, Dawn!
Just *who* is the mysterious "Mr X" who's been sending threatening notes to Dawn and phoning her while she's babysitting, *alone*?

No 3: Mallory and the Ghost Cat
Mallory thinks she's solved the mystery of the spooky cat cries coming from the Craine's attic. But Mallory can *still* hear crying. Will Mallory find the *real* ghost of a cat this time?

No 4: Kristy and the Missing Child
When little Jake Kuhn goes missing, Kristy can't stop thinking about it. Kristy makes up her mind. She *must* find Jake Kuhn . . . wherever he is!

No 5: Mary Anne and the Secret in the Attic
Mary Anne is curious about her mother, who died when she was just a baby. Whilst rooting around in her creepy old attic Mary Anne comes across a secret she never knew . . .

No 6: The Mystery at Claudia's House
Just what is going on? Who has been ransacking Claudia's room and borrowing her make-up and clothes? Something strange is happening at Claudia's house and the Babysitters are determined to solve the mystery . . .